MEET THE GIRL TALK

Sabrina Wells is petite, with curly auburn hair, sparkling hazel eyes, and a bubbly personality. Sabrina loves magazines, shopping, sleepovers, and most of all, she loves talking to her best friends.

Katie Campbell is a straight-A student and super athlete. With her blond hair, blue eyes, and matching clothes, she's everyone's idea of little miss perfect. But Katie has a few surprises for everyone, including herself!

Randy Zak has just moved to Acorn Falls from New York City, and is she ever cool! With her radical spiked haircut and her hip New York clothes, Randy teaches everyone just how much fun it is to be different.

Allison Cloud is a Native American Indian. Allison's super smart and really beautiful. But she has one major problem: She's thirteen years old, five foot seven, and still growing!

Here's what they're talking about in
Girl Talk

KATIE: Um, Sabs. I don't think I'm going
            to the playoff party.

SABRINA: Why not?

KATIE: Well, Jean-Paul invited Stacy to
            the party!

SABRINA: What! Why did he invite her?

KATIE: I guess, he thought she was my
            best friend or something.

SABRINA: Hey! If I can find a way so Stacy
            won't be at the party, will you go?

KATIE: I don't know. What do you have in
            mind?

FAMILY AFFAIR

By L. E. Blair

GIRL TALK® series created by Western Publishing Company, Inc.

Produced by Angel Entertainment, Inc.

Western Publishing Company, Inc., Racine, Wisconsin 53404

Text by Crystal Johnson

Chapter One

I woke up with a start at the sound of my alarm clock buzzing loudly. I reached over to the night table next to my bed and pressed the top of the clock until the buzzing stopped. Slowly, I stretched. Then I pushed back the covers, lowered my feet onto my soft pale blue carpet, and wiggled my toes.

It was six-forty-five. Good. I probably had just enough time to get into the shower before everyone else. I looked out my bedroom window and frowned at the cold Minnesota rain. I wished it was still cold enough to snow. Then I could go ice-skating with my best friends, Sabrina Wells, Allison Cloud, and Randy Zak.

Then I remembered it was Monday morning and a school day. I turned away from the window with a sigh. I didn't have time to worry about the rain outside. Instead, I'd better take my shower right away, or I'd be late for school.

I couldn't believe that it had only been a month since my mom had remarried. It was even harder to believe that only two weeks ago my mom's new husband, Jean-Paul Beauvais, and his son, Michel, had moved in with Mom, Emily, and me. Now our house was totally packed! The basement was stuffed with most of the Beauvaises' furniture. Michel was sleeping in the guest room, and the family room had thousands of cardboard boxes and wooden crates scattered all over the place. I couldn't even watch TV without having to move something out of my way. But the worst of it was the bathroom situation. Five people living in a house with only one bathroom was a total pain.

Suddenly I heard my sister, Emily, open her bedroom door. Knowing Emily, I had to move fast or I'd have to wait ages to get into the bathroom. I grabbed my pink bathrobe and ran into the hallway. Just as I got to the door of the bathroom, Emily jumped in front of me.

"Emily!" I cried. "I'd probably get more bathroom time if I moved in with Sabs! Even if she does have three brothers at home, at least they've worked out a schedule!"

"Relax, Katherine. I just need the hair

dryer," my sister said. I hate it when she calls me Katherine. She knows I like being called Katie instead.

Emily leaned over and grabbed the hair dryer from the cabinet under the bathroom sink. Then she turned and disappeared into her bedroom. When she left, I closed the bathroom door tightly and let out a long breath of air.

Now it was my turn for a nice long hot shower. I turned on the faucet and stepped into the shower stall. I screamed and leapt away from the icy stream. Goose bumps popped out all over my skin. Shivering, I spun the knobs again. This was the third time in two weeks that there was no hot water! Everyone else must have taken their showers and used up all the hot water. I made up my mind right then and there that if I was going to survive in this family, I was going to have to get up an hour earlier every morning — probably for the rest of my life!

My hair was already wet, so I grabbed the shampoo, gritted my teeth, and stepped back into the freezing water. I think it was the fastest shower I ever took in my life.

Two minutes later I stood in the middle of the bathroom wrapped tightly in my terry-cloth bathrobe. I tried to stop my teeth from chattering as I looked around for a towel to dry my hair. The only dry one I could find was a little hand towel. I stared hopelessly at the tiny thing, then started rubbing my long, dripping hair with it. It would just have to do.

Of course, the towel was soaked within seconds. I flung it into the hamper and opened the bathroom door to go to Emily's room. I decided I'd get warmer once I dried my hair with the hair dryer. I was just about to knock on her door when she flung it open.

"Stupid thing!" she muttered, frowning at the hair dryer in her hand. "It overheated." Emily thrust the dryer at me. Then she turned on her heel and went back into her room.

I looked down at the useless dryer in my hand. It was always overheating, especially now that five of us were using it. I began to wonder what else would go wrong today!

There was nothing else I could do but get dressed while I waited for the dryer to cool down. Going to my room, I put the dryer on my dresser and pulled open my sweater drawer. I decided to wear my new pink sweater with my favorite jeans. I grabbed a pair of matching pink socks out of my sock drawer, which I keep organized by color, and carried the clothes over to my bed.

After I dressed I tried the dryer one last time. Luckily, this time when I flipped on the switch, it worked. I finished drying my straight blond hair, and then I pulled it back and fastened it with a pink satin hair clip.

Finally I was all ready. I even had fifteen minutes to spare until I had to leave for school. Gathering my books from my desk, I ran downstairs to the front hall to put them in my backpack.

"K.C.! I am glad you're here. Do you know where your mother put the box my sweaters are in?"

Michel, my new stepbrother, was wearing jeans and a T-shirt. He stood in the middle of a huge mound of clothes in front of the hall closet. Besides the boxes in the family room, some of his clothes were hanging in the front hall closet, since the closet in the guest bedroom is so small. I stared down at the mess in amazement. I couldn't believe what a disaster Michel had just created.

I didn't know where to begin looking for his sweaters. "Sorry, Michel, I don't know," I told him. "Did you ask my mom?"

"She's not downstairs yet. Oh, well, this will do." Michel bent down and pulled a sweatshirt from the rubble. Then he shoveled the mess back into the closet with his foot and pushed the door shut.

I raised my eyebrows and turned toward the kitchen. I definitely didn't want to be around when Mom opened *that* door. She's a total neat freak.

I like Michel a lot, but living with him is totally different from just being his friend. He and I have been in seventh grade together at Bradley Junior High ever since he moved here to Acorn Falls from Canada with his father a few months ago. I got to know him because we both play on our junior high school hockey team.

I zipped my books into my backpack and decided to grab something to eat. Opening the kitchen door, I saw Jean-Paul standing by the stove surrounded by food.

Not only is it strange getting used to having a brother after having only a sister for thirteen years, it's also pretty weird having a new father. Especially since my real dad died just three years ago.

Jean-Paul has this thing about cooking us a hot breakfast every morning before he leaves for the office. Mom loves it because she doesn't have to cook and she thinks it's really romantic that her new husband cooks for her. I guess I wouldn't mind except that Jean-Paul is used to cooking for himself and Michel, who both happen to eat *a lot*. He makes tons of food! I glanced over to the kitchen table. It was loaded with pancakes, toast, Canadian bacon, scrambled eggs, orange juice, and milk.

Michel came into the kitchen right behind me and immediately started piling food on a big plate. I usually don't eat a big breakfast on school days. I just like to have a bowl of oatmeal or something. Besides, today had already started out so crazy that I wanted to get to school on time.

"Good morning," I said as I grabbed a glass of juice and a piece of toast.

"*Bonjour*, Katie!" Jean-Paul greeted me with a smile, his dark eyes crinkling at the corners.

It's easy to tell that Jean-Paul and Michel are related. They're both tall, with thick dark hair. My best friend Sabs thinks Michel is really cute.

"Mon Dieu!" Jean-Paul continued in his heavy French-Canadian accent. "You have to start the day with more to eat than that."

Jean-Paul and Michel are always telling me I don't eat enough. Luckily, the phone rang right then, and my eating habits were temporarily forgotten.

"Hello!" Jean-Paul said, answering the phone. "Uh-huh . . . So the contract is signed?"

I wasn't really listening. I didn't want to eavesdrop. Besides, Jean-Paul is always talking about contracts and business. He owns an advertising agency.

"Très bien! I'll talk to you later. *Au revoir."* Jean-Paul hung up just as Mom and Emily walked into the kitchen.

"Good morning, everyone," Mom said, smiling. She practically glowed with happiness, the way she has ever since she met Jean-Paul. She didn't even seem to mind that the house was so crowded and messy.

"Who was that calling so early?" Mom asked, giving Jean-Paul a peck on the cheek.

"Good news, Eileen. The deal for the Wingers went through," Jean-Paul said, hugging Mom.

"The Minnesota Wingers?" I asked, growing excited. I love hockey, and the Wingers are my absolute favorite professional hockey team.

"*Oui*. I didn't want to mention it until my offer was accepted, but now it is final. I have bought the Minnesota Wingers!" Jean-Paul announced.

"*Bought* them?" Emily asked, as if she thought she hadn't heard right.

When Jean-Paul nodded, Michel jumped up and yelled, "Yay! That's wonderful!"

I guess Michel must be used to his father being rich and buying and selling things. It was still pretty incredible for Emily and me, though.

"I'm glad everyone's here," Mom said, pausing to give us all a big smile, "because Jean-Paul and I have some more exciting news for you." Mom poured herself a cup of coffee and stood next to Jean-Paul, who was cleaning up the stove.

All of a sudden I got a funny feeling in the pit of my stomach. The last time Mom and Jean-Paul got us all together to make an announcement, it had been to tell us they were planning to get married. That had been a big shock. What changes were they planning to make now?

Chapter Two

I looked from Michel to Emily. I could tell that neither of them had a clue. Glancing down at my watch, I saw that it was eight o'clock. My first class started at eight-thirty. Whatever the news was, I hoped it was brief. I wanted to have some time before class to tell my friends about Jean-Paul buying the Wingers.

"Your mother and I think we have found a new home for us to live in," Jean-Paul told us, putting his arm around my mother.

I stared at them both in shock. What were they talking about? We already had a home to live in.

"*Fantastique!*" Michel burst out. He looked totally thrilled about the news.

"Don't worry," my mother said cheerily, looking directly at me. "We haven't signed anything yet. We want you all to come look at the house with us this evening. If it meets everyone's approval, we'll tell the real-estate agent to go ahead and start the paperwork."

Emily sat quietly looking down at her plate. I knew exactly what she was thinking. We had lived in this house all of our lives. I *liked* living here. I couldn't imagine living anywhere else. I mean, I definitely thought that something had to be done about the crowded situation in this house, but I had never actually thought about moving.

"Where is this new house?" Emily asked warily.

I hadn't thought of that. What if it was really far away? What if I had to go to a different school? I turned to look at Mom anxiously.

"It's over on the other side of town, on the corner of Granite Springs Drive and Stone Hill Road," Mom explained.

"Wow! All the houses there are huge! Isn't that right near the Acorn Falls Country Club?" Emily asked. She was obviously very impressed.

Mom nodded. "Yes, and we'll be just a few blocks away from that nice girl Katie skated with in the Winter Olympics, Laurel Spencer. And we're not too far from the Hansens', either."

I didn't think *that* sounded so great. Who

wanted to live near Stacy Hansen, the principal's daughter and the biggest snob in the whole school? Besides, that neighborhood was miles away from where we lived now and from where all my friends lived.

"And since the new house is farther away from school, you won't be able to walk every day," Jean-Paul jumped in. "So Emily will have to drive Katie and Michel to school in her own car. That is, if you don't mind, Emily," Jean-Paul teased.

"You mean I get my own car!" Emily cried, jumping out of her chair.

Mom nodded. "I pick up my new car today, and then you get my old one."

Emily ran over to Mom and Jean-Paul and hugged them so hard she almost knocked them over. Personally, I kind of liked walking to school, except on rainy days like today. But Emily had been wanting her own car ever since she got her driver's license earlier this year.

"*Très bien!*" Michel burst out. "When do we move?" he asked.

The family announcement was over now, and Mom and Jean-Paul started talking about house things. Emily ran to call her boyfriend, Reed, and tell him about her car. Michel was still eating his second helping of pancakes and eggs. I decided to leave before Michel so I would have some time alone to think about what moving would be like.

Saying good-bye, I grabbed my knapsack and umbrella and walked quickly through the rain to school. Ten minutes later, I was standing in front of my locker, shaking the last drops of water off my umbrella. I still didn't know what to think about moving into a new house.

"Katie!"

I looked up to see Sabs running down the hall toward me, dragging her hot-pink umbrella on the floor behind her. Her long red curly hair was even curlier than usual because of the rain. "You won't believe what I heard on the radio this morning!"

"Hi, Sabs," I greeted her. Sabs has some kind of earthshaking news almost every day. I'm used to it.

Sabs peeled off her pink raincoat and hung it in our locker. We've been locker partners ever since the beginning of the school year.

"I had the radio on this morning while I was getting dressed, and the sports news came on,"

14

Sabs said, talking in this big rush. "Anyway, I wasn't really listening until the announcer said, 'Jean-Paul Beauvais.' Katie, why didn't you tell me he was buying the Minnesota Wingers?"

"He only told us about it this morning. I was going to tell you, honest," I told her.

"Boy! This is *so* exciting!" Sabs squealed.

"What's *sooo* exciting?" Randy asked as she and Allison walked over to us. Randy was dressed in all black, right down to her socks and boots. Needless to say, black is her favorite color. I guess black clothes are really popular in New York City, where Randy used to live before she moved here with her mom at the beginning of this school year.

"Hi, Katie. Hi, Sabs," said Allison. Allison looked really cute. She was wearing a burnt-orange miniskirt and a gold sweater covered with orange and red flowers. She wore matching burnt-orange tights and these really cool black ankle boots. Her long shiny black hair was held off her face by a yellow headband, and her arms were filled with a stack of library books.

"Jean-Paul is buying the Wingers," Sabs said, answering Randy's question.

"Cool! They're pretty good, aren't they?" Randy asked. Randy is a diehard New York Rangers fan, but I think she's starting to get into the Minnesota teams, too.

"Well, they're number one in the Continental Hockey League now, because they won last night's game," Allison said proudly.

Al must have a photographic memory or something. She reads the paper from front to back every morning before school and can remember everything in it. I wish I remembered things that easily. It would definitely cut down on study time.

"Wow! Good old J.P. must have some big bucks to buy a whole major-league team," Randy said. "What exactly does he do for a living again?"

"He owns a big Canadian advertising company. He inherited it when his father died," I answered.

Al was looking at me kind of funny. "You don't look very excited, Katie. Is anything wrong?" she asked. Al is really perceptive. Somehow she can always tell exactly what you're feeling.

"Yeah, Katie. Aren't you psyched?" Randy

put in. "You love hockey, and now you can have rinkside seats for every game!"

"And you'll get to meet all those cute hockey players!" Sabs squealed. She was so excited she was actually jumping up and down.

"Yeah, I guess . . ." I began. I was just about to tell my friends that we were moving and how I was kind of upset about it when Laurel Spencer and B. Z. Latimer walked over. They are both part of Stacy Hansen's clique, which doesn't really get along with my group of friends at all. Actually, Laurel and B.Z. are pretty nice when Stacy the Great isn't around. Laurel and I even sort of became friends when we were skating partners during the Winter Olympics.

"Hi, neighbor!" Laurel said, smiling at me. "My mom told me this morning that you're buying the old Higgens mansion. That's only about six blocks from our house."

I nodded and tried to smile. Just then the bell rang for first-period class, and Laurel and B.Z. hurried off to class. When I looked back at my friends, I could tell they were in shock.

"What! You're moving?" Sabs cried, staring at me with her mouth open.

"Into a *mansion?*" Randy added, raising her eyebrows.

"Why didn't you tell us?" Allison asked quietly.

My friends looked a little hurt that I hadn't said anything. And now there wasn't any time to explain because we were all going to be late for class!

I felt as if my head was spinning. I just wanted to crawl into my locker and never come out again.

Chapter Three

"What time did you say Emily was picking us up?" Sabs asked the following Monday afternoon right after school. She was sitting next to me on a bench in front of Bradley Junior High. Al and Randy were on my other side.

"She said she'd be here at three," I answered.

"It's already a quarter after," Randy pointed out, looking at her Day-Glo watch.

"I hope she gets here soon. I just can't wait to see this place," Sabs said with a sigh.

"Besides," Randy added, "we must have watched every kid in the whole school walk by while we've been waiting for Emily."

I couldn't believe how psyched my friends were to see the new house. Fortunately, they had been really understanding when I explained that I hadn't told them about the new house because I hadn't known about it myself.

Mom and Jean-Paul signed the papers for the house last Friday. Mom decided to take today off to meet with painters, floor polishers, rug layers, chimney cleaners, telephone installers, and all kinds of people who were helping her get the house ready for us to move into in just twelve days. I was kind of surprised when I asked if my friends could come after school to see the house and Mom said yes. I think Mom is really excited about moving.

Last Monday evening the whole family piled into Jean-Paul's car and went to see the house just like Mom promised. It was awesome! The first thing you saw to the right and slightly behind the house was the stables. Mom said I could get a horse once we got settled. Another nice thing was a little pond I could go ice-skating on in the winter.

The house itself was really huge — four stories high, with seven bedrooms, five full bathrooms, and a powder room off the foyer on the first floor. Also on the first floor were the kitchen, dining room, living room, and family room. The family room had a connecting half-bathroom. There was even a library with a small connecting office and half-bathroom, for Jean-

Paul to work in. I had never seen so many bathrooms in my life!

Emily was all excited because she got the top floor to herself. It was really the attic, but the previous owners had turned the space into a bedroom, sitting room, and bathroom for their live-in servant. It was small, but Emily would have the whole set of rooms to herself. Secretly, it was the best news I'd heard all day. I was thrilled not to have to battle Emily for the bathroom anymore.

The good feeling didn't last too long, though, because I found out that Michel's and my bedrooms, were on the third floor with a connecting bathroom between the rooms. Now I was going to have to share a bathroom with a boy. Yuck!

Mom and Jean-Paul's bedroom was absolutely the most incredible room in the whole house. It was actually two rooms that took up an entire half of the second floor! Mom called it a suite. I couldn't help but think how weird it was that Mom's new bedroom is bigger than the living room we have now.

When you first walked into the room, I mean suite, you walked into a sitting room. In the middle of one wall were french doors that opened out to a balcony. When you walked through a door on the opposite side of the room, you went into the bedroom. It had two separate walk-in closets and a connecting bathroom with a Jacuzzi bathtub.

Suddenly Allison interrupted my thoughts. "Isn't that your mom's car?"

I stopped thinking about the new house and looked in the direction Al was pointing. I saw our blue four-door car pull into the school driveway.

"It's Emily's car now," I told her. In fact, now Mom was driving a brand-new red sports car that Jean-Paul had bought for her.

"It's great that Emily has a car. Now maybe I won't have to bribe Luke to drive us everywhere," Sabs said, getting up from the bench.

"Are you still washing his car every weekend to pay for the last time he drove us to the Widmere Mall?" Randy asked.

Sabs nodded, rolling her eyes. Her older brother always acts like it's a total pain to take us anywhere.

"Sometimes I'm glad I'm an only child," Randy said just as Emily pulled up in front of us. I could hear music playing loudly inside the car before I even opened the door.

"Hi, Em," I shouted over the radio.

Emily reached over and turned the music down while my friends and I climbed in. "Hello, girls." She tries to act so mature all the time, but she's only three years older than I am. "We have to get over to the new house right away. Mom said the interior decorator was arriving at three."

Sabs's hazel eyes lit up. "An interior decorator? This is so exciting! When I'm a famous actress, I'm definitely going to have my house done by an interior decorator."

"I don't know if I'd want someone else to decorate my house," Allison said. "I'd want to do it myself so it would be exactly the way I like it."

Personally, I felt the exact same way, but Mom said Jean-Paul did a lot of entertaining for business and needed the new house in order right away. She also said that Mrs. Gold, the decorator, was famous for getting a house ready in a very short amount of time. At least I was going to be allowed to pick out the colors for my new room. That was why I had to meet

Mom there today.

"Look! That must be it!" Sabs cried, bouncing up and down in the backseat. She pointed at the huge brick house with the "Sold" sign still sticking out of the front lawn.

Emily drove up the tree-lined brick driveway and parked in front of the five-car garage, next to Mom's car and another car I didn't recognize. We all jumped out of the car. Emily ran inside, but the rest of us stood in the middle of the circular driveway, staring at the house. It really *was* beautiful, but I just couldn't shake the feeling that I was here on vacation or something. This place wasn't very homey or cozy, the way our old house was.

"Wow!" Sabs exclaimed, looking everywhere all at once.

Randy was staring back toward the stables. "I would *love* to have my own horse," she said.

"Are those tennis courts?" Al asked, pointing to the fenced-in clay courts behind the house.

I nodded, really happy that my friends had come with me today. They were so excited that it started to rub off on me. "Come on inside, you have to see my new room!" I told them.

24

I ran past a row of manicured bushes in front of the house to the massive wooden front door. I pushed on the big brass handle, and the heavy door swung slowly open. Judging by all the noise inside, I could tell a lot of the workmen were still there.

My friends followed me inside and looked around. Sabs stared at the crystal chandelier hanging from the eighteen-foot-high ceiling in the entry hall and said, "Everything is so big!"

"What's in there?" Allison asked, pointing to the two sliding wooden doors off the foyer. They were partially open, and through them I could see a man dressed in white overalls guiding a big noisy floor polisher across the wood floors. I decided we'd better not go in there now.

"Mom calls that the parlor, but I call it the living room," I answered. "Come on, we can go up the back stairway to my room. Maybe Mom's there," I added, stepping carefully around a ladder one of the workmen had left in the foyer.

We practically had to walk through the whole first floor to get to the back stairs. I stopped in the wood-paneled dining room to show my friends the fireplace and the french doors that led to the slate patio, the herb garden, and the greenhouse.

"I feel like I'm on a museum tour with school," Allison said, giggling as she looked around.

All Sabs kept saying was "Wow!" and that made the rest of us giggle. It took a lot for Sabs to use just one word.

"This is the kitchen," I said as I stepped onto the black-and-white-tiled floor.

Randy walked over to the stainless steel stove, which has eight burners and two ovens. "You could make some great Thai food on this thing," she said. Randy is really into exotic foods.

"Maybe we can make some when we have a sleep-over here," Al suggested.

"If the maid or the cook isn't preparing all the meals, that is," Randy said in this fake snobby voice.

"We're not going to have maids or cooks," I said automatically. At our old house Emily and I took turns vacuuming and dusting every week. Even though this place was a lot bigger, I just assumed we'd have the same arrangement.

"Is your mom going to quit her job now that she doesn't have to work?" Allison asked.

"No, she likes to work," I answered. In fact, Mom had just gotten a promotion. Now she was in charge of the whole loan department at the bank, and she was really excited about it.

Sabs nodded dramatically. "I can understand that. No matter how rich I become when I'm an actress, I'm sure I'll always keep working just for the love of acting," she said.

"Well, I hope you remember us, the little people in your life, when you're so rich and famous," Randy teased.

"Of course I will! Look, Katie hasn't changed, and she's rich now," Sabs said.

It sounded really weird to hear Sabs say that. "I am not rich!" I defended. I guess I always thought that rich people were snobby and conceited, and I knew I didn't want to be like that. Besides, Jean-Paul was the one who had a lot of money, not me.

"Katie! Is that you?" I heard Mom's voice coming from the back stairway off the kitchen. "Come on up. Mrs. Gold needs you to look at a few color samples."

I led my friends up the back stairs, not telling them that they were called the servants' stairs. I mean, I really didn't want people to think I was going to turn into a snob.

After going up two flights of stairs, we

were upstairs in the wide, empty hallway that led to the two bedrooms that would be mine and Michel's. The stairs continued up to Emily's room on the fourth floor. It was definitely a workout climbing up all those stairs, but I guessed I would get used to it.

I looked down the hall to see a very blond woman wearing a purple cape and carrying piles of carpet and wallpaper samples. She swished down the hallway toward us, coming upstairs from Mom and Jean-Paul's room one floor below. My mom was right behind her.

"Good, you're here," Mrs. Gold said. "We're ready to start the children's rooms." She swept past me and flung open the door to my room. I nearly gagged from the strong smell of her perfume. I didn't dare look at Al, Sabs, and Randy as we followed Mrs. Gold and Mom into my room. I knew if I did, I would crack up.

"So which one is yours," Mrs. Gold asked Mom, looking at the group of us.

I stepped forward and raised my hand slightly. "I'm Katie."

Mrs. Gold barely nodded at me and then walked quickly around the room. "What a lovely space!" she said.

I eyed the huge, bare room again, hoping it would look nicer than it did the other night when I had first seen it. It didn't. The windows were still bare, and the large space seemed just as cold and empty as it had before. The only difference was that now the walls were dotted with plaster and there were drop cloths all over the floors.

"Mauve!" Mrs. Gold suddenly burst out. The rest of us turned to look at her. "This room just cries out for mauve!" she announced.

Mrs. Gold was off again, her fingers flying through the huge book of wallpaper samples. "Now, for the walls . . ." she began, pausing at a sample that looked kind of like the finger painting that Al's seven-year-old brother, Charlie, had done in his first-grade art class.

I jumped in before this went any further. "Actually," I began, kind of loudly. Mrs. Gold was a hard woman to get through to. "I really wanted white wallpaper with little pink rose-buds on it. And a baby-blue carpet," I added quickly before the mauve idea came up again. I wasn't even sure what color mauve was, but I knew I didn't want it in my room.

"But, dear —" Mom actually spoke for the

first time since Mrs. Gold had swooshed into my new room and taken over. "That's exactly what your old room looks like. Wouldn't you like something different?"

Isn't having this room — this whole house, for that matter — different enough? I thought to myself. But I knew I couldn't tell my mom that, so I just said, "No, Mom. I like rosebuds and blue."

Mrs. Gold let out this big sigh. I hoped that meant she was giving in. "Well, I guess I can work with the wallpaper." She flipped through the giant book again. "Here." She thrust the page out for my mom to see, and I craned my neck to look. "Laura Ashley has a rosebud print wall covering with a corresponding wallpaper border, bed linens, and window dressings. If that's what the girl wants . . ." She let her voice trail off and looked at me over her glasses.

"She acts like *she's* going to live here," I heard Randy whisper behind me. Luckily, Mrs. Gold was so busy ranting about the carpet color that she didn't hear.

"But I just *cannot* work with baby blue!" Mrs. Gold said the words "baby blue" as if they totally repulsed her. "Now, this 'Seafoam' would work wonderfully with the mint leaves on the wallpaper."

She pointed to a green rug sample that she pulled out from under the giant wallpaper book. Dropping the piece of rug by my feet, she said, "I'll pencil it in, hon. You think about it."

Then she was off through the bathroom that connected my room to "the boy's room," as she referred to Michel's room.

"Seafoam? It looks more like mold to me!" Sabs said, staring down at the light green carpet sample lying on the floor. Then her hand flew to her mouth. "Ohmygosh, Katie. I'm sorry! It's really not that bad."

"That's okay, Sabs," I told her. "I was thinking the exact same thing."

"I'm sure you can talk to your mother later. After all, she makes the final decision, not Mrs. Gold," Allison assured me.

I hoped Al was right, but I was still worried.

Chapter Four

I couldn't believe how quickly the next twelve days passed. Before I knew it, it was moving day. On Saturday morning I sat in the middle of my bedroom, surrounded by boxes. It was so weird that everything I'd accumulated in my life fit into a roomful of boxes.

I glanced at my night table to see what time it was, but then I remembered that my alarm clock was already packed in one of the large cardboard boxes labeled "Katie's Bedroom."

"Katie! The moving truck will be here in half an hour. Are you ready?" Mom called from the stairway. She had taken all of last week off from work. Somehow, between Mrs. Gold, who worked with the painters and carpenters, and the people Mom hired to pack up most of the stuff in our old house, she had gotten the new house ready — even the attic and the basement!

"Almost done, Mom!" I called back. I pulled open the final drawer of my dresser and began to transfer the neatly folded sweaters into an empty flowered cardboard storage box. Mom had bought several pretty cardboard boxes to move my clothes in. She said I could always use them for storage in my new walk-in closet.

I finished quickly and fitted on the box lid. Then I just stood there and looked around my room.

All my posters were rolled up in cardboard tubes, leaving bright spots where they had hung on the faded wallpapered walls. My books were packed away, too, and my mattress lay bare on the bed. The dresser and my desk and wall unit were totally empty.

It was weird. I mean, this room had been the most special place in the world to me for my whole life. Now I was going to leave it, just like that.

Suddenly I knew that if I didn't get out of there right away, I would start crying. I glanced around one more time to make sure I hadn't left anything and then walked into the hall and shut the door behind me.

"K.C.!" Michel called as he bounded up the

stairs, two at a time. He had on his favorite pair of ripped jeans and a polo shirt I thought I remembered him wearing yesterday.

"Do you know where is the tape for the boxes?" Michel asked. I hoped that meant that he was done with his packing, too.

I nodded and led the way to the kitchen, where Mom had left the packing tape and a pair of scissors for us to use. "Are you almost finished?" I asked, handing him the tape.

"*Oui*, but I need your help," Michel said.

I followed Michel into the family room and stopped short at the doorway. "Michel! You've hardly packed anything!" I cried, looking around at the piles of clothes on the floor.

"Yes I have," Michel said. "Look, I packed that crate there." He pointed to a milk crate that held some books, his hairbrush, and his toothbrush. I couldn't believe he called that being packed!

Michel began to shove the piles of clothes into a cardboard box. He kept going until it was totally overflowing. "K.C.! Could you come and step on this so I can tape it shut?" he asked, using all his strength to try pushing down the flaps of the box.

I looked at him skeptically but stepped up onto the overstuffed box anyway. I held my breath, waiting for it to burst.

"Jump up and down a little," Michel instructed, still trying to get the flaps to close. I bounced lightly. "*Bien!* It is done!" Michel cried triumphantly. I let out a sigh of relief and jumped off the box.

"Oh — you forgot this," I said, bending to pick up a sweatshirt that was partly hidden under the couch.

"No problem!" Michel shoved the sweatshirt into the crate, right on top of his toothbrush. Yuck!

Soon after that, the movers arrived. The next few hours passed in a whirlwind. Four moving men whizzed through the house and managed to fit everything neatly into the moving van. Even Michel's boxes made it in one piece! I managed to capture my cat, Pepper, during all the confusion. With her safely in her cat cage, we were ready to move on to the new house. Before I knew it, I was standing in the driveway in front of the huge brick house.

Mom and Jean-Paul were inside, directing the men where to put things. Emily was already up in her room talking on the phone to her boyfriend, Reed. I didn't know where Michel was, but I figured he was somewhere inside.

I plopped down on Michel's beat-up old trunk and waited for it to be my turn to show the movers where to put my boxes.

"I am so excited!" said Michel, coming out of the front door and sitting next to me. "A new house, two new sisters, and a new mother!"

I looked around at my neatly packed boxes, and then at Michel's mess. I still wasn't sure how I felt about my new family, but one thing was for sure. Having a new brother was definitely going to be an interesting experience!

Chapter Five

The following Tuesday afternoon I was sitting in front of Bradley Junior High with Sabs, Randy, and Allison, waiting for Emily again.

"Where is she?" I said under my breath, looking down the school's driveway for Emily's car.

The past weekend had been crazy with unpacking boxes and moving furniture in the new house. At last my family was pretty much settled in, so I asked Mom if my friends could come over after school. I said it was because I wanted them to see my new room, but mostly I wanted them there because it was really weird being in a new house. Things at home still felt really different.

Emily was already fifteen minutes late picking us up. Yesterday she had been even later. It looked like I would be spending a lot of time on this bench. I was glad that my friends didn't seem to mind. In fact, Sabs was really into this story she was telling.

". . . So when I took the carrots out of my bag during study hall, Stacy said, 'Oh, is that how you get your hair that color?' Then she and Eva laughed all period," Sabs told us, her red curls bouncing. "My hair is auburn, not bright red! I can't believe how mean she is."

"Don't worry about what Stacy says, Sabs," said Allison. "She's just jealous."

"Yeah. She was probably showing off for Eva 'Jaws' Malone and the rest of the Stacy clones," Randy added.

At that exact moment Stacy, Eva, Laurel, and B.Z. came out the school's front door and walked toward us. Of course, my friends and I started cracking up.

"Katie, do you need a ride home?" Laurel asked me when she got closer. Even though Laurel is part of Stacy's clique, she and I get along okay. She's been really friendly since I had moved so near to her house.

Stacy grinned at me, but gave Randy, Al, and Sabs a really snotty look. "But I'm sure there's not enough room for *everyone* in the car," she said, flipping her long blond hair over one shoulder. She walked away toward Laurel's sister's car, with Eva behind her.

"Thanks, anyway, Laurel. Emily's coming," I said, totally ignoring Stacy.

Laurel looked a little embarrassed at the way Stacy was acting. She and Eva and B.Z. quickly said good-bye and followed Stacy into the car.

Sabs stared after the car as it drove away. "Oooh, she makes me so mad! How can she be so mean all the time?"

"What goes around comes around," Randy said with a shrug.

"What's that mean?" Sabs asked, crinkling up her nose.

"It means that one day all the mean things Stacy does will come back to haunt her," Allison explained.

Randy nodded. "Yeah, like one day when she makes that horrible face — you know, the one she does when she's being a bingo head — her face will just stay like that forever!"

Randy did a perfect imitation of Stacy's snotty expression, and I laughed until my sides hurt. It felt really good being with my friends.

Turning to Allison, I asked, "How's your

mom doing?"

A few weeks ago, Al found out that her mother is having another baby. I think she felt kind of weird about it. After all, Al and her brother, Charlie, have been the only kids in the family for the last seven years.

"She's all right," Al replied. "She gets tired a lot now, so I try to help out around the house as much as I can."

"Hey, here comes Emily!" Sabs said. She jumped up off the bench and grabbed her knapsack from the ground. "You're so lucky to get driven home every day. Luke would never drive me."

I looked at Sabs in surprise. I liked walking home; I never realized that she didn't.

"Really! I wish I could catch a ride on snowy days when I can't skateboard. By the time I walk to school, I feel like an ice cube!" Randy added. She climbed into the backseat between Sabs and Al and put her skateboard between her legs.

"Where's Michel? Doesn't he need a ride home today?" Allison asked, glancing back at the school.

I shook my head. "He's going over to Scottie's house after school to catch the Wingers game on the cable TV sports channel. Our cable isn't going to be hooked up until tomorrow," I explained.

"I read this morning in the paper that if the Wingers win today's game, they make the play-offs," Allison informed us.

"The New York Islanders aren't going to make it this year, but the New York Rangers have a shot!" Randy put in.

"If the Rangers play against the Wingers in the interleague finals, who would you cheer for, Randy?" Sabs asked.

I turned around in the front seat to hear what Randy would say. I mean, she's been living in Acorn Falls for some time now, but she still has her dad and her friend Sheck back in New York.

Randy didn't say anything for a second. "Well, I guess I'd go for the Wingers," she finally decided. "Especially since they're Jean-Paul's team now."

Sabs, Al, and I started cheering. I guess we were all happy that Randy had finally settled into life in Minnesota. For a while we were afraid she might move back to New York and live with her father. I guess if Randy could get used to her parents' divorce and move to a different state, a new house, and a new school *and* make new friends, I could get used to a new house.

"Who's that man?" Sabs asked when we pulled up in front of our big brick house. She pointed to a gray-haired man who was clipping the bushes in the front yard.

"He's the new grounds keeper," I said, feeling a little uncomfortable. "Jean-Paul hired him yesterday. He's going to live in the apartment above the garage."

"Grounds keeper?" Randy echoed, raising an eyebrow at me.

Sabs looked as if she was going to die. "Wow! First the interior decorator, and now a gardener. Gosh, Katie, you're so lucky!"

I didn't feel very lucky. In fact, I felt totally embarrassed. I had told my friends that things weren't going to change just because Jean-Paul was rich, and now we had this gardener. I didn't know how to tell them we had a housekeeper, a cleaning lady, and a cook, too.

So many things had changed. Mom used to love to garden, and Emily and I had always helped rake the leaves at our old house. Mom had hired our neighbor's son to mow the lawn, but that was it.

I opened the car door and waited for my friends to pile out of the car before I began walking toward the house. When we went past the gardener, he bowed his head slightly and said, "Good day, young ladies."

Randy made this dramatic bow and said "Good day" right back to him.

"I feel like a princess or something!" Sabs whispered, giggling. She and Al looked kind of embarrassed.

I could feel myself turning bright red, so I just walked to the front door and reached for the doorknob. Before I could grab it, the heavy door swung open and there stood the housekeeper. She had black hair and was wearing a black skirt and a white blouse.

"Good afternoon, Miss Katie," she said. "Your mother told me to expect you and some friends today. I've set out some milk and cookies in the kitchen for you. The cook started today. She baked some cookies this afternoon." The woman held the door open and stepped aside so we could come in. I definitely did not feel comfortable being called "Miss Katie."

"Is my mom home?" I asked her.

"No, miss. She's working late today," the housekeeper answered politely. Then she led us through the dining room to the kitchen.

I had forgotten that since Mom got this promotion, she'd be working late a lot. I still thought that Emily and I could handle dinner and cleaning on our own, though.

Sabs, Randy, and Allison all gasped as we went through the dining room. There was an oriental rug in the middle of the shiny parquet wood floor. Jean-Paul had shipped this big antique dining room set from Canada — a long table with twelve matching tapestry chairs. There was a china cabinet, too, and a sideboard filled with silver. Jean-Paul had also bought an antique brass chandelier that used real candles instead of those light bulbs that look like flames. A big oil painting of Paris hung above the fireplace, and the french doors were hung with these white lace curtains that I thought were really pretty.

"Did anyone call when I was gone, Mrs. Smith?" Emily asked the housekeeper when we got to the kitchen. She didn't seem to be having a problem with this servant business at all.

"Yes, Miss Emily. Reed called for you. He will be picking you up at four," Mrs. Smith told her. Emily thanked Mrs. Smith and ran up the back stairs to her bedroom while my friends sat down at the kitchen table.

Sabrina grabbed a chocolate cookie off the plate in the middle of the table. "Mmm, these are still warm. Don't you want one, Miss Katie?" Sabs said, giggling.

"In a minute. I have to feed Pepper," I said. I went to get a can of cat food from the shelf, but Mrs. Smith stopped me.

"I did that already, miss. Adorable cat you have," she told me.

For a second I just looked at her. I had been feeding Pepper every day after school since first grade. Now I couldn't even take care of my own cat anymore! Sitting down with my friends, I grudgingly took a cookie and bit into it. I had to admit it was good.

I was still chewing my first bite when a short, heavy woman with a stern face and graying hair walked into the room. She was dressed all in white and wore a slightly stained apron tied around her wide waist. I figured this had to be our new cook.

"Hi, did you make these cookies? They're great!" Sabrina said cheerfully to her.

The woman answered Sabs with a kind of grunt and a nod.

"Hi, I'm Katie," I said. I waited for the woman to say something, but she barely nodded at me. "I live here," I went on. I felt silly having to explain that, but I figured maybe she didn't know who I was.

Again I only got a nod. Finally I just asked her, "What's your name?" I don't think I would have had the nerve to be so direct if my friends hadn't been there. This woman looked like she could be the evil villain in one of those horror movies Randy is so crazy about.

"Everyone calls me 'Cook,'" the woman answered shortly. She then took out a big butcher knife and began to chop up a head of lettuce. Randy started giggling, and I knew she had to be thinking about horror movies, too.

I guess my friends didn't feel comfortable around the cook, either. We all sat there munching on cookies and not saying anything. At last Allison said, "Hey, can we see your room now?"

"Sure," I replied.

We all put our empty milk glasses in the sink, then went up the servants' stairs to my new room. Little did I know the day Mom told me these were called the servants' stairs that we would actually have servants!

Then a terrible thought hit me: These servants wouldn't be living here, too, would they? We did have three spare bedrooms! I'd have to ask about that right away.

Sabs, Al, and Randy hadn't seen my new room since the day when Mrs. Gold was here. I thought it looked a lot better now. I swung open the door and stepped back so my friends could see.

I had to admit, my new room was pretty great. I had kept my old desk, bookcase, dresser, and, of course, the dollhouse my dad had made me. But Mom and Jean-Paul had bought me a new brass four-poster canopy bed. It had a matching daybed that I could use as a sofa during the day, or for when my friends slept over.

Sabs ran into the room and looked around. "You have your own TV in here!" she exclaimed.

Allison walked over to the window seat and peeked out the pink-and-white-striped curtains. "You're going to love your window seat. I sit in mine to read all the time. Look, Ran. You can see the stables and the pond from here!"

"Cool," said Randy, going over to look out the window. Then she plopped down in one of the two white wicker chairs Mom had ordered from Mrs. Gold for me. The cushions were covered in the same rosebud print that was on the wallpaper. "I'm glad to see you didn't go for the mold-green carpet!" Randy commented, looking down at my pale blue carpet.

I nodded. "I got Mom to change the order with no problem."

"Didn't Mrs. Gold die?" Sabs wanted to know, flopping down on my bed.

"Yeah, I thought she wouldn't use baby blue!" said Al.

"Actually, this color is called 'Summer Sky,'" I told my friends. Sitting next to Sabs, I reached over to pet Pepper, who was asleep on the end of the bed. I was glad that at least one of us had adjusted to the move with no problem.

"Well, it looks like baby blue to me." Randy laughed.

"I know, but don't tell Mrs. Gold!" I said, giggling. This was really starting to feel like *my* room, especially with my friends in it.

"Hey!" Sabrina cried, jumping up suddenly. "Can we see Michel's room?"

"I don't know." I hesitated. Michel's room is right next to mine, through the adjoining bathroom. But I wasn't sure we should go in there. I mean, I wouldn't want Michel and his friends looking at my room if I wasn't here.

"Come on, just a peek. Please? He'll never know," Sabs begged.

I could tell Al and Randy were curious, too. "Well, okay." I finally gave in. "But just for a second. And you can only look through the bathroom door!"

We all went into the bathroom. Luckily, it's really big, so we didn't have a problem fitting in.

"I can't wait to see what Mrs. G. did in there," Randy said, rolling her eyes.

Actually, I was kind of interested to see Michel's finished room myself. As of yesterday, it was still packed with boxes. Come to think of it, I had left a few boxes still packed in my room this morning. I wondered who had unpacked them. I also wondered how I would find anything after someone else had put things away.

I opened the door to Michel's room a crack, and all four of us peeked through. Michel's comforter had a red and navy blue plaid pattern, with navy blue pillowcases that matched the dark blue curtains on his windows. His rug was a thick navy blue one, and his two dressers, desk, and chair were all made from the same dark wood. The walls were paneled in dark wood, too. The room looked really dark, but it was kind of cozy and definitely masculine. No one would ever get Michel's and my rooms mixed up, that was for sure!

"Not bad," Randy commented. "I expected much worse from that decorator."

Suddenly we heard voices. The next thing I knew, Michel's door flew open! Grabbing the doorknob to the bathroom door, I pulled it shut as quickly as I could.

"Oww!" Sabrina cried. "My hair!" Then I noticed that I had slammed the door on a clump of her hair, and she couldn't move. I opened the door an inch, pulled Sabs back into the bathroom, and closed the door again. I hoped that the guys had been too busy talking to notice.

"That was a close one!" Randy whispered.

Just then the bathroom door flew open and

Michel stood there staring at us. "What are you guys doing in the bathroom?" he asked, looking confused. Scottie Silver and Flip Walsh, friends of Michel's and mine from the hockey team, were right behind him.

I opened my mouth but couldn't think of a good excuse. I definitely couldn't tell Michel we were looking at his room without permission!

"I told you girls are weird," Flip said, shaking his head at us.

Scottie peeked over Flip's head and waved. "Hi, you guys," he said.

I happen to think that Scottie Silver is really cute. We've gone out a few times, but mostly we're just friends.

"K.C., you should have seen the game. It was *incroyable!*" Michel said excitedly. Luckily, he seemed to have forgotten about what my friends and I were doing in the bathroom.

"It's over already?" I asked, looking down at my watch.

Michel nodded. *"Oui.* The Wingers won! We're going to the playoffs! I called my father at his office, and he's getting us tickets to the first home game!"

"Hey, and don't forget your friends," Scottie

said, poking Michel in the side.

"That's the best part," Michel continued. "My father said we could invite all our friends and have a party before the first game at the arena. It will be in one of the private boxes. We can even meet the team!"

"Wow!" Sabs cried. "I can't believe it!"

"Cool!" Randy agreed at the same time as Al said, "That sounds fun."

I definitely agreed with my friends. I had been feeling so weird about moving to this house that I had pretty much forgotten about Jean-Paul's buying the Wingers. But this play-off party was something I could get really excited about.

Chapter Six

The next day at school, everyone was talking about the Wingers making the playoffs. The cafeteria was already totally packed when Sabs, Randy, Allison, and I got off the lunch line, trays in our hands. I heard the words "Wingers" and "playoffs" coming from a couple of tables.

Wednesday is pizza day in the Bradley cafeteria, so I had told Cook that I'd buy lunch today instead of bringing it from home. I think she was kind of insulted. I reminded myself to make sure to tell her how good dinner was last night, to make up for it. I was relieved when Mom told me that Mrs. Smith and Cook weren't going to live with us, but it was still really weird having strangers in the house cooking and cleaning. It would take a while to get used to it.

I looked around the crowded lunchroom. We were a little late, since Al had stayed after

English class to hand in a poem she had written for Bradley's literary magazine.

"Oh, wait! I think I see some seats over there," Sabs said, pointing at a table by the window.

"Forget it, Sabs," Randy said, frowning. "Stacy's sitting there with her clones. I'd rather sit on the floor than eat with them."

I kind of agreed. Besides, I knew that Stacy would die before she'd let us sit at her table.

I couldn't believe it when, two seconds later, Stacy stood up and waved at me. I turned around to see if she was waving at someone behind me, but I didn't see anyone.

"Hey, Katie! Come sit with us!" Stacy cried, shooting me a big smile.

For a few seconds, we all just stood there in shock. Why was Stacy suddenly being so nice to me? She usually went out of her way to be nasty to me and my friends.

Allison finally broke the silence. "We might as well, guys. If we don't sit down soon, lunch period will be over."

"I hope I don't choke on my lunch!" Randy muttered as we walked across the room to Stacy's table.

"I saw the moving van in front of your new house this past weekend, Katie. Welcome to the neighborhood," Stacy said to me as we sat down. She was talking in this really fake sweet voice.

Actually, Stacy doesn't live in our neighborhood. Her house is a few miles away, and it isn't as big as ours. I didn't say anything, though. I didn't want to be as snobby as she was.

Stacy totally ignored my friends and kept talking to me about the new house and how wonderful it would be if we could car-pool to school some days. I just nodded and hoped she would be quiet soon. Finally Eva started telling her this story about some cute guy in her class, so I had a few minutes of peace.

"I never thought she'd shut up!" Sabs whispered to me, leaning across the table.

"I wonder what caused this sudden good-neighbor policy?" Randy asked.

Just then the cafeteria got even noisier. Looking up, I saw that the whole hockey team had come into the cafeteria. The guys were all slapping each other on the back and talking excitedly.

"They sure look happy about something!"

Randy commented.

"Michel is probably telling them about Jean-Paul's hockey party," I said.

I guess Stacy heard me, because she broke off from talking to Eva. "Party? Did you say you're having a party?" she asked me.

"It's not my party, it's Jean-Paul's," I told her, feeling a little annoyed that she was interrupting my conversation with my friends.

"Oh, you must mean the big Winger playoff game party. I think I heard Scottie talking about it this morning. It sounds really fun," Stacy said, with another one of her phony smiles.

"It's not a *big* party, Stacy," I told her.

Then it hit me. Suddenly I knew why Stacy was being so nice to me. She wanted me to invite her to the playoff party!

For the rest of the period, my friends and I sat quietly and let Stacy and her clones talk. Luckily, the bell rang pretty soon, and we were able to get out into the hallway and talk.

"Boy, does she have a lot of nerve!" Randy said, shaking her head.

Al nodded. "Does she really think you're going to invite her because she's pretending to be nice to us?" she asked.

"I don't know, but I know I'm not going to invite her," I said determinedly.

"Hey, don't forget we're going to Fitzie's after school today," Sabs reminded me. "That should be really fun. We haven't gone there since you moved." I could tell she was trying to cheer me up.

Actually, I was looking forward to it. Fitzie's is the greatest place to hang out. All the kids from Bradley Junior High go there. It's kind of far from our new house, though. I miss hanging out there with all the kids from school. So today I'd asked Emily if she could pick up Michel and me there at four-thirty, and she said it would be fine.

"Thanks for reminding me!" I told Sabs and smiled. It was a pain having to plan things so far ahead of time so I could tell Emily when and where to pick me up. I really missed being able to walk home whenever I wanted to.

"Hey, Katie. I meant to tell you before, your clothes are totally cool today," Randy told me when she, Sabs, Al, and I were walking to Fitzie's after school.

I looked down at my outfit, puzzled. What

could I be wearing that would make Randy notice? I mean, her style of dressing is a lot wilder than mine.

"Ohmygosh!" I cried when my eyes got down to my feet. I had on a pink sweatshirt and pink sneakers, which I was wearing with my white jeans. But instead of pink socks, I had accidentally put on orange ones!

"I grabbed the wrong socks!" I explained, bending over to pull the bottom of my jeans lower over my socks. Emily had been rushing me this morning, and it was hard enough lately finding anything, since the housekeeper puts my clothes away for me.

"No, really. It's the new look. Totally psychedelic and sixties! All you need is to add something lime green," Randy suggested.

"I think the yellow headband is cool with the pink and the orange," Sabs pointed out.

"Yellow?" I reached up to touch the headband. "But I thought it was white!"

Al gave me a reassuring smile. "Don't worry, Katie! No one will notice, I'm sure."

I could tell my friends were trying not to crack up. It *was* kind of funny, I had to admit. I would definitely have to start laying my outfits out the night before.

When we walked into Fitzie's a few minutes later, I could see that a lot of kids from Bradley were already there. We spotted an empty booth in the back and headed for it.

"Hi, Katie!" someone said to me from a booth we passed. I looked over and recognized a boy who had been in my science class last year. I couldn't figure out why he was saying hi to me all of a sudden, but I said hello back.

"Hey, Campbell! Great news about the Wingers!" another guy I hardly knew called out. I vaguely remembered him from hockey tryouts at the beginning of the year. He didn't make the team, and I didn't even know his name. I wondered why he remembered mine. I guessed it was because I was the only girl who tried out. "Got any extra tickets?" the boy asked.

I was too shocked to answer. I couldn't believe it! All anybody wanted from me was those stupid hockey tickets. I was beginning to wish Jean-Paul had never bought the Wingers!

"Katie! Over here!" I heard someone else call. *That* voice I did recognize, but I wished I didn't. It was Stacy. I turned to see her shoving

Eva over in their booth to leave a small space for me to sit.

"No thanks, we have a table," I answered, trying to stay calm. I was getting totally sick of all this. Did Stacy really think that I didn't know she was only being nice to me to get invited to the playoff party?

Sabs grabbed my sleeve and pulled me over to our booth. "Don't let it bother you, Katie," she told me.

"Hi, guys," someone else said, walking up to our table. Frowning, I spun around to see who it was now.

Then I saw the smiling, freckled face of Sabs's twin brother, Sam, and I totally relaxed. Finally someone who actually liked *me* and not just my hockey tickets!

Sam was with his friends Nick Robbins, Arizonna, Billy Dixon, and Jason McKee. All those guys are pretty nice, and I didn't mind a bit when they squeezed into the booth with us. It was definitely a tight fit, though.

"I don't believe you guys missed the game yesterday," Sam told us. "It was great! You should have come over to Nick's and watched it with us."

"That's okay. Michel saw it at Scottie's, and

he told me everything, play by play," I said, glancing at the board on the wall to see what the ice-cream flavor of the day was.

Nick gave up trying to take off his jacket in our cramped booth. "I can't wait for the playoff party," he said excitedly.

"Totally cool, dudes! I hope I'm invited. It'll be my first real Minnesota party," Arizonna said.

Sabs gave the guys this killer look. "Stop bothering Katie about the playoff party, okay?"

"I don't mind, Sabs," I told her. "Of course all you guys are invited. I really want all of Michel's and my real friends there. The problem is that *everybody* wants to come. They just don't understand. Jean-Paul is nice enough to give us this party, but I don't want to take advantage of him and invite everybody in the whole school."

I rolled my eyes when I heard Stacy's fake voice calling out again, "Michel! Over here!"

I turned around and saw Michel just inside the door. Of course he went over to talk to Stacy.

"That bingo head never gives up!" Randy said.

"Stacy could never miss the biggest party of

the year without putting up a fight. You can be sure of that!" Sabs predicted.

I looked back at Michel, who had just squeezed into Stacy's booth and was smiling and laughing with her. I was afraid Sabs was right about Stacy. And it looked as if Michel was falling for her tricks.

Great. Now I had a brother who was friends with my least favorite person in the entire world!

Chapter Seven

"Sabs! Are you sure we have to do *all* this stuff at once?" I cried into the phone receiver on Thursday night.

"The article in *Belle* says we have to if we want to get the full spa makeover in only an hour," Sabs answered matter-of-factly.

According to Sabs, this makeover was supposed to "banish the late-winter blues," or something like that. All I knew was that with everything that had happened lately, I was ready for a new me. I just wasn't sure this was the way to get it.

I was sitting on a little brass stool in my bathroom, dressed in my old pink bathrobe. My hair was wrapped up in a towel, a mud mask covered my face, and I had toilet paper stuffed between my toes. I stretched to polish the nail of my big toe, trying not to drop the phone.

"This is hard to do!" I cried. The towel started to slip over my eyes, and I squirmed to push it back without ruining the pale pink fingernail polish I had just put on.

"Keep trying," Sabs encouraged, "or you'll never be able to deep-condition your hair and get a manicure, pedicure, and facial in an hour like the article says." She was sitting at the phone downstairs at her house doing the same thing I was.

I heard a loud clattering in my ear. "Sabs?" I said, but she didn't answer. She must have been having trouble doing all those things at once, too.

I sighed and looked at Michel's muddy sneakers lying in the corner while I waited for her to pick up again. Maybe I could give *him* a makeover. I was really happy that the cleaning lady who comes three days a week cleaned our bathroom. But I still always ended up picking up after Michel.

Sabs came back on the line. "Sorry about that, Katie. Thirty-two more minutes and you can wash out your conditioner. Your nails should be dry by then. Is your face mask getting hard yet?"

Thirty-two more minutes! That sounded

like forever! I gingerly touched my face to feel if the mud mask was drying.

"I guess so. It feels kind of cracked," I answered. I looked around the bathroom. The one thing that it didn't have was a clock. "What time is it?" I asked.

"About four-thirty," Sabs told me. "We'll be done with our makeover by five."

I hoped so. It felt like I had been in this bathroom a very long time. I was enjoying the privacy, though. It wasn't easy to get time alone with a family of five, all of our friends, and a bunch of servants.

"I want to go upstairs to the bathroom and see how I look. I'll call you back in twenty-nine minutes," Sabs said quickly.

"Okay, bye," I answered and hung up the phone. It was hard to believe we actually had a phone in the bathroom. It felt really cool.

I didn't know what I was going to do for the next twenty-nine minutes, especially with my wet nails. I should have remembered to get some magazines out of Emily's room. But then I remembered that it was a magazine that had gotten me into this mess!

"*Bien!* I'll get the towels," I heard Michel say

in his bedroom.

I stood up in a panic. I couldn't let him see me like this!

"Get three. Brian and Flip need towels, too."

Oh, no! That was Scottie's voice! I stood up in a panic. Michel was going to come in here to get towels, and they would *all* see me looking like this.

I ran for the door that connected the bathroom to my bedroom, but it was too late. The bathroom door leading to Michel's room opened, and Michel came running in.

He stopped short when he saw me. *"Mon Dieu*, K.C. What have you done to yourself?" Michel asked.

Then Brian and Flip walked in. They started to laugh so hard that they practically fell on the floor. Michel tried to hold it in, but then he burst out laughing, too.

I wished I could have crawled down the drain and disappeared. But then it got even worse. Scottie walked in! He just stood there for a minute with his mouth hanging open. He didn't even laugh, he just looked really shocked. "Katie?" he said, as if he wasn't sure it was me. How embarrassing!

"Hi, Scottie," I mumbled, staring down at the floor. I definitely could not bring myself to look at him. But then I noticed how stupid the toilet paper between my toes looked!

"We were just going to use the equipment in your exercise room. Got to keep in shape for hockey season, you know," Scottie quickly explained. He sounded almost as embarrassed as I felt. "Come on, you guys. Let's get the towels and go." Scottie shoved Brian and Flip out the door.

Michel was still laughing as he grabbed a pile of towels from the closet. "K.C., you have to warn me next time you're going to do this," he said, then walked back into his room.

"Why don't you warn me before you come busting into my bathroom!" I cried. I slammed the door behind him, then leaned against the door and blew out a long, slow breath.

I almost died when I caught a look at my reflection in the mirror. I hadn't realized how funny I actually looked. With the "seafoam-green" towel around my head and mud all over my face, I guess I did look kind of like the Creature from the Black Lagoon. Still, the more I thought about Michel walking in on me like that, the madder I got.

I had to do something about this bathroom situation, I decided, and right now. I didn't even stop to wash my face. Walking as fast as I could with the toilet paper still stuck between my toes, I just ran downstairs to Jean-Paul and my mother's suite.

The door was open, so I walked into the sitting room. "We have to talk!" I said. I wanted to sound serious, but my voice came out sounding squeaky and high.

Mom looked up from the papers she was reading and smiled. "Talk about what, Katie?" she asked.

"Mom, you have to do something about Michel! He just walked right into the bathroom with half the hockey team and he didn't even knock!"

"Katie, I'm sure Michel didn't think you were in there, dear," Mom said logically.

I was getting more and more frustrated. How could she act like it was no big deal? "But, Mom," I tried again. "Michel didn't even bother waiting to find out if I *was* in the bathroom or not. What if I was in the bathtub or something?"

"I'll talk to Michel about knocking before he goes into the bathroom," Mom said. She paused and gave me this serious look. "But, Katie, you are going to have to get used to having a brother. All of us have had to make adjustments."

Adjustments! Emily had her own car and the whole top floor of the house to herself, including her own bathroom and her own phone. Mom had been walking on air ever since the wedding, and Michel seemed thrilled with this whole new family thing. It seemed to me that *I* was the only one making adjustments around here, and now Mom was acting like I had no reason to be upset!

Everything that had happened in the past few weeks had really gotten to me. Strangers kept coming up to me to ask for tickets to the hockey playoffs. And then yesterday after school, Stacy came over and started acting like she and Michel were best friends. I ended up spending the whole afternoon in my room.

I felt the tears welling up in my eyes. Finally I just couldn't hold it in anymore.

"How come you are always sticking up for Michel?" I shouted. "He's not even really your son!"

The minute I said the words, I was sorry. Mom's face went pale. Then it got even worse. I turned and saw Jean-Paul standing in the doorway. He must have heard what I had just said about Michel.

I didn't know what to do. I just turned and ran until I reached my room. Going to the bathroom, I rinsed off all the conditioner and mud. Then I flopped down on my bed and let myself cry. Finally I calmed down and got dressed in a jeans skirt and pink blouse.

A little while later, someone knocked at my door. When I opened it, the gardener was standing there.

"Hello, miss," he told me. "Mr. B. sent me up to install locks on the bathroom doors."

I blinked in surprise. Why hadn't I thought about locks? It was so simple! I thought it was nice that Jean-Paul had sent the gardener to put in locks for me. It was really nice of him. All of a sudden I felt really embarrassed and sorry about what I'd said.

I showed the gardener the bathroom and then made my way downstairs to find Mom and Jean-Paul. I didn't exactly know what I wanted to say, so I took my time going downstairs.

"Katie, your friend Stacy is here!" Jean-Paul said cheerfully as I walked slowly into the foyer. He and Mom were both standing in the hall with Stacy. Mom was holding flowers.

Just the sight of Stacy with her fake smile made me mad. I didn't even try to be polite.

"She's Michel's friend, not mine," I said simply, crossing my arms. "He's at the pool."

Jean-Paul's face fell, and Mom looked totally horrified. They would never understand what a terrible person Stacy really was. Michel sure didn't. My mom left to show Stacy to the stairs that led to the pool room in the back of the house.

Before leaving the hall, Stacy stopped and turned back to Jean-Paul. "Thank you so much for the invitation to the party and for your hospitality, Mr. and Mrs. Beauvais," she said. She smiled sweetly at me and then walked away.

"What!" I spun around to face Jean-Paul. Now I was *really* upset. "How could you invite her?" I cried.

"She's a lovely girl. I thought it would be nice to invite your friend," Jean-Paul said calmly.

"What do you know! She only wants to be

my friend because you bought that stupid hockey team!" I cried.

Just then Mom walked back into the room. "Katie! How can you talk to Jean-Paul like that?" she said angrily. "He bought us this house and he's having that party just for you and your friends! He's doing his best to be a good father to you."

I could feel myself start to cry again. "I didn't ask for this house or for a new father!" I shouted. "And forget about the party — I'm not going!"

"Katie!" Mom cried. She stood there for a minute without saying anything. Then she glanced at her watch and said, "Jean-Paul and I are meeting some people for dinner, so we'll have to talk about your behavior later. Now, go to your room, young lady!"

I wouldn't look Mom in the eyes, but as I turned to go upstairs, I caught a glimpse of the hurt expression on Jean-Paul's face.

I knew I'd been acting badly lately, but they just didn't understand what was going on. No one understood.

I went to my room and waited until I heard Mom and Jean-Paul leave for dinner. Then I picked up the phone and dialed Sabs's number. Now I had to tell her I wouldn't be going to the party. This had been one of the worst days of my life!

Chapter Eight

Katie calls Sabrina.

SAM:	Hello, the White House!
KATIE:	Hi, Sam. Is Sabs there?
SAM:	Katie! Way to go, Wingers! Saturday night's game is going to be awesome.
KATIE:	Yeah. Is Sabs there?
SAM:	Sure. Blabs! Phone! Did you get that gook off your face?
SABRINA:	Oh, shut up, Samuel! Hello?
KATIE:	Hi, Sabs.
SABRINA:	Katie! I'm sorry I didn't call you back before. My brothers came home just as I was about to wash off my mud mask, and Sam is being a total jerk about it.
KATIE:	Michel walked in on me, too. Um, Sabs. I don't think I'm going to the party anymore.

SABRINA: Why not? I thought we had it all planned.

KATIE: Well, I kind of had a fight with Mom, and I think I'm in trouble.

SABRINA: She said you couldn't go? What did you do?

KATIE: She didn't actually say I couldn't, but she was pretty mad.

SABRINA: What happened?

(Katie sighs.)

KATIE: First Michel, Flip, Brian, and Scottie walked in on me in the bathroom. Then I accused Mom of favoring Michel. Then Jean-Paul invited Stacy to the party, and I said I didn't ask for a new father and that I'm not going to the party.

SABRINA: What! Ohmygosh, Katie, Scottie saw you like that? And Stacy's coming to the party now? Why did Jean-Paul invite her?

KATIE: You know how she's been hanging around Michel lately, and she even came over with flowers for

Mom. I guess when she came over again today, Jean-Paul thought she was my best friend or something.

SABRINA: I'm sure your mom and Jean-Paul will forgive you, Katie. I mean, they must know it's hard for you to get a new house and a new family.

KATIE: *(quietly)* But I'm not sure I want to go now. Especially if Stacy's going to be there.

SABRINA: Well, if you're not going, then I'm not going, either.

(There is a short pause.)

SABRINA: Hey! If I can find a way so Stacy won't be at the party, will you go?

KATIE: Sabs, how can you do that? You know she would never miss the party.

SABRINA: Well, if I can do it, will you go?

KATIE: I don't know. What do you have in mind?

SABRINA: It's a surprise. Listen, I'm going to work on a plan. See you tomorrow at our locker, okay?

KATIE: Okay. Bye.

SABRINA: Bye.

Sabs calls Randy.

RANDY: Yo!

SABRINA: Hey, Ran. It's Sabs. We've got a
            problem.

RANDY: Problems are my game — shoot!

SABRINA: Stacy the Great got herself invited
            to the playoff party, and now
            Katie doesn't want to go.

RANDY: Stacy's such a bingo brain. How
            did she get invited?

SABRINA: Jean-Paul invited her. She got him
            to believe that she was really
            good friends with Katie and
            Michel.

RANDY: I guess you can't blame J.P. He
            probably doesn't know what a
            fake she is.

SABRINA: Stacy even brought over flowers
            to Mrs. Campbell — I mean, Mrs.
            Beauvais.

RANDY: It figures. So what are we going to
            do?

SABRINA: Well, I have a plan.

RANDY: Uh-oh. Acorn Falls, look out!

SABRINA: No, really. I bet anything it will stop Stacy from coming to the party. I need you and Al to help, okay? But let's keep it a surprise for Katie.

RANDY: Good idea. Besides, we don't want Jean-Paul to think that Katie went behind his back to uninvite Stacy or anything.

SABRINA: Definitely not. So, anyway, tomorrow in science class, you and Al start talking about the party, right? But make sure Stacy overhears you.

RANDY: No problem. Then what?

SABRINA: Then you and Al talk about how much fun it will be, since Jean-Paul has just changed it to a costume party, with prizes for the most outrageous costume!

(Randy laughs.)

RANDY: I get it. Stacy will show up in this wild costume and be so embarrassed when she's the only one dressed up that she'll leave!

SABRINA: Exactly!

RANDY: Cool! But wait, Sabs. Won't Stacy talk to other people and find out it's really *not* a costume party?

SABRINA: When will she have time? Science is your last class, right? And tomorrow is Friday. The game is Saturday night. Besides, the only people who are invited are you guys and Michel's guy friends. You know, Sam and the hockey team. We can tell those guys to go along with it.

RANDY: You're right, this might just work.

SABRINA: Come to school early tomorrow so we can work out the details. Oh, and call Al and tell her?

RANDY: Sure thing. *Ciao!*

Randy calls Allison.

ALLISON: Hello, Allison speaking.

RANDY: Hey, Al. Listen, Sabs just called and said Katie isn't going to the playoff party because Stacy conned J.P. into inviting her. Katie talked to Sabs, and I guess she's pretty upset.

ALLISON: I don't blame her. Everyone is trying to get her to invite them, even people she hardly knows.

RANDY: We've all been so psyched about the party, I guess we didn't realize what Katie's been going through lately. I mean, I'd freak if M got remarried and we had to move again!

ALLISON: So what should we do to help her?

RANDY: Sabs has this plan to make sure Stacy doesn't stay at the party. She figures then maybe Katie will change her mind.

ALLISON: I hope she does. But what if Katie still doesn't want to go? Then I think we should all stay home with Katie and have our own party. I mean, we're her real friends.

RANDY: Good idea!

ALLISON: I'll ask my mom if we can have the party at our house.

RANDY: Anyway, Sabs want us to come to
           school early tomorrow so we can
           talk about her plan.
ALLISON: Great! See you then.
RANDY: *Ciao!*
Allison calls Katie.
KATIE: Hello.
ALLISON: Hi, Katie. It's Allison. I heard
           what happened, and I'm calling
           for all of us to say that we'll
           always be your friends and it
           doesn't matter if you have money
           or hockey tickets. We still love
           you. If you do decide not to go to
           the party, we'll just stay home
           and watch the game with you.
           We'll have our own party. Okay?
KATIE: You guys would really miss the
           party?
ALLISON: Sure! It wouldn't be fun without
           you, anyway.
KATIE: Thanks, Al! You guys are great!
ALLISON: So are you! So I'll see you
           tomorrow at school, okay?
KATIE: Okay. Bye.
ALLISON: Good-bye.

Chapter Nine

"Knock, knock!" Emily said softly as she pushed open my bedroom door.

I had just gotten off the phone with Allison and I was feeling a tiny bit better. It was nice to know that if I did decide not to go to the party Saturday, or if Mom wouldn't let me, I could still count on my friends.

I felt horrible about hurting Jean-Paul, though. And I knew that I would have to talk with Mom sooner or later about how I'd behaved.

"Come on in, Em."

Emily looked great, as usual. She was wearing a new navy-blue-and-white polka-dotted shirt with a navy miniskirt. She had bought them with the money Grandma Campbell had given us when she came to visit for Mom and Jean-Paul's wedding. I put my money away in my piggy bank, since there wasn't anything I wanted at the time.

"What's up?" Emily asked.

"Nothing," I answered. I didn't think Emily would understand why I was upset. She seemed so happy in this new house with Jean-Paul and Michel.

Emily hesitated for a minute and then said, "I thought I heard some yelling before. Did you and Mom have a fight?"

When I didn't say anything, Emily walked across the room and sat next to me on my bed. "Do you want to talk about it?" she asked.

All of a sudden I couldn't hold it in anymore. "I can't stand that Jean-Paul is rich and we had to move! I hate sharing a bathroom with Michel! He's a total slob and walks in on me with the guys. At school, everybody wants to be friends with me just because I have playoff tickets! Stacy Hansen is coming to the playoff party and is always hanging out with Michel now! And the cook scares me!"

I blurted it all out at once. I realized I wasn't making much sense, but that's how I had been feeling lately, like nothing made sense.

I waited for Emily to give me a lecture. Instead, she put her arm around me and said,

"Katie, I know exactly how you feel. I thought I would love having my own car, but now I have to get up earlier and rush every morning to drop you and Michel off and then rush in the afternoon to get you before cheerleading practice. Not that I mind driving you, but everything was easier before, when Reed used to just pick me up for school."

I guess she didn't have it too easy lately, either. Being totally responsible for getting two kids to and from school on time had to be a lot of work.

"And those playoff tickets!" Emily went on. "It's all Reed can talk about lately. Hockey, hockey, hockey! I'm sorry, I know you must be looking forward to it, but — "

"Looking forward to it?" I cut in. "I don't have any time to get excited with everyone in the school asking me for tickets, even total strangers!"

Emily nodded. "Reed's friends started that, too. I just told them all no. That's all you have to do, Katie. Just tell everybody you don't have any tickets for them, and they'll leave you alone."

Emily made it sound as if that was the easiest thing in the world. But she didn't know Stacy Hansen!

"Besides, the playoffs won't last forever," Emily said. "Now, about Michel. Have you told him how his mess in the bathroom bothers you?" she asked.

I glanced at the closed door to the bathroom. I could hear Michel taking a shower inside. "No," I answered. "But I did tell Mom, and she told me that's just how boys are."

"First of all, you have to realize that Mom is very busy now with her new position at the bank," Emily told me. "Not to mention a new house and a new husband and son. She doesn't have time to play referee between you two."

I hadn't really thought about that.

"Second, how is Michel supposed to know that it's bothering you if you don't tell him?" my sister continued. "He's not a mind reader, you know. You have to talk to him about the bathroom situation and ask him to respect your privacy. And then if he leaves his dirty clothes in the bathroom again, just push it all into his room as a little reminder."

I nodded my head. She was right, I really hadn't talked to Michel at all lately. I just got mad at him and complained to Mom.

"Do you feel any better about things now?" Emily asked.

I shrugged. There was still the problem with Stacy, Jean-Paul, and my inevitable talk with Mom.

Emily gave me a little hug. I guess she sensed that I was still feeling a little down. "Why don't you come downstairs with me and see what Cook made for us to eat," she suggested. "Jean-Paul and Mom are out for dinner, so we can eat in the family room and watch movies on the VCR, if you don't have homework to do."

Actually, I hadn't eaten since lunch at school, and my stomach was starting to grumble. "I finished my homework during my free period at school today," I told her. I jumped up off the high bed and started for the door.

"I hope Cook made something normal for dinner. If I eat one more French thing, I think I'll start talking like Jean-Paul and Michel!" Emily said, following me.

I laughed. Emily and I don't always get along so great. But tonight it was nice being with my sister.

"Hello, Cook. Katie and I would like to eat now," Emily instructed Cook when we reached the kitchen. I was really impressed that Cook's grumpy attitude didn't seem to scare her at all.

Cook nodded and took two casserole dishes out of the oven, placing them on a tray. "Careful, they're hot," she instructed, and went back to cleaning a pan at the sink.

I carefully picked up the tray and headed for the family room.

"I'll grab the forks and napkins. You go pick out a movie," Emily told me.

Our new family room is definitely my favorite room in the house, besides my bedroom. It's the only room downstairs that isn't filled with antiques and doesn't look like a museum. Mom had picked out a huge comfortable beige leather couch and thick off-white carpeting. They look really good with the marble fireplace. There's also a stereo and a big-screen TV with a VCR built right in, and a whole cabinet of newly released movies that Jean-Paul got because his company does the advertising for some big movie chain. We even have a pool table in the back of the room with one of those hanging brass and green glass lamps over it, like in the movies. Michel and his friends love that.

After I found a movie, I popped it into the VCR. I set the tray down on the coffee table, then opened up two wooden snack tables and put them in front of the couch so Emily and I could eat there.

"So what's for dinner?" Emily asked, gesturing at the casserole dishes.

I lifted the lid with a napkin and peeked inside. "Yum! Homemade macaroni and cheese. But what's that green stuff in there?" I asked, frowning.

"Broccoli," Emily said, looking over my shoulder. "You know how Cook feels about having vegetables every day."

"Well, it looks good anyway," I decided. Putting the lid back on, I walked back to the VCR to start the movie that I'd picked out for us to watch.

Michel had homework to do, so he ate dinner up in his room. Emily and I watched two movies, and before I knew it, it was time to go to sleep. Mom and Jean-Paul weren't home yet, so I went to bed.

The next day was Friday. I woke up for school as usual, except this time, instead of complaining to Mom about Michel hogging the bathroom, I just asked him if I could brush my teeth before he took a shower. He said sure, and everything went smoothly.

Mom had an early meeting at the bank and didn't join us for breakfast. I only saw Jean-Paul for a minute before I had to leave for school. He acted like nothing had happened, so I did, too. I guessed my talking-to got pushed off a little further.

Actually, I kind of wanted to get it over with. I hate when Mom's mad at me. And I still felt awful about hurting Jean-Paul's feelings.

I grabbed my lunch bag off the counter, and Emily drove Michel and me to school. But this time she didn't yell at us to hurry up and I made sure I was ready early so Emily wouldn't be late for high school.

When I got to school, I found Sabs, Randy, and Allison waiting for me at Sabs's and my locker. They all looked concerned. I had forgotten that when I talked to them on the phone the night before, I had been pretty upset about everything.

"Hi, guys," I greeted them. I hung my knapsack on the coat hook and then hung up my denim jacket over it.

"Is everything okay now?" Sabs asked. She was wearing this really cute flowered jumper with a long-sleeved white T-shirt underneath.

I shrugged. "I guess so. I haven't talked to Mom yet, and Jean-Paul hasn't said a word about yesterday."

"I know things will work out," Al said, smiling.

"Yeah, these things just take time," Randy agreed.

I thought it was really considerate that my friends didn't ask what I had decided about tomorrow's party, even though I knew they were dying to go.

"You guys, I decided that if I'm still allowed to, I'm going to the playoff party," I told them.

"Great!" Sabrina said, hugging me. "If you're really sure, that is," she added quickly.

I nodded. "I wish Stacy the Great wasn't going to be there," I added. "I'll just have to try to ignore her."

When I said that, Sabs, Randy, and Allison gave each other these funny looks.

"What are you guys up to?" I asked.

"I have a feeling Stacy won't be staying long at the party," Sabs told me, starting to giggle.

"Just leave everything to us!" Randy added.

I was getting really curious now. "Come on, guys! What is it?"

I turned to Allison, hoping I could get the secret out of her. But Al just shook her head and said, "You'll have to wait until tomorrow!"

"We're not going to tell, so just get your books for class and let's go," Sabs ordered.

Suddenly she gasped and grabbed my arm. "What are we going to wear tomorrow? I totally forgot to plan my outfit!" Sabs exclaimed.

Just then the warning bell rang, so we all headed for our classes. It was hard to concentrate on schoolwork for the rest of the day, though. I kept wondering what my friends were up to.

Chapter Ten

It was after three o'clock when I left school to meet Emily. As soon as I burst through the door, I found myself standing smack in front of Stacy, Eva, and Michel.

"Michel, are you sure you don't need a ride home? It's really no problem. My mother will be here any second," Stacy was saying.

"*Merci*, but my sister will be here soon," Michel told her. "K.C.! *Bonjour*," he called when he saw me. "Are you coming home with me and Emily today?"

I nodded. The minute Stacy saw me, she turned her head away and pretended I wasn't there.

"There she is," Michel announced. He pointed to Emily's car, which had just pulled up in front of the school. "See you later," he told Stacy and Eva.

"*Au revoir*, Michel!" Stacy called after him.

I almost gagged. How could Michel not see what a fake she was?

I really wanted to tell Michel that I was sure Stacy was only being nice to him because she wanted to go to the party and because he was rich. But Michel was so excited about tomorrow's game that I decided not to say anything until after the playoffs. Besides, maybe she would leave him alone after the party and I wouldn't have to say anything at all.

The whole way home in the car, Michel talked about the game and the party and all the people who were going to be there.

"Michel, how many people did you invite anyway?" I asked him.

"Not too many. Only Sam, Nick, Jason, Billy, Arizonna, and the whole hockey team," Michel counted off on his fingers.

That sounded like a lot of people to me. I had only invited Sabs, Randy, and Allison. I knew Emily had invited Reed and his best friend, Ron. Then again, I didn't know how big a party Jean-Paul was planning.

"Are you sure Jean-Paul won't mind?" I asked. "I thought we were only inviting our best friends."

Michel gave me this surprised look. "Those *are* all my best friends. *Ça ne fait rien.* It does not matter. My father loves big parties!" he told me.

I figured he knew what Jean-Paul liked and didn't like better than I did, so I turned back around in the front seat of the car.

"Did you invite Laurel?" Emily asked me.

I shook my head. "I thought about it, but I didn't invite her because I didn't want to invite Stacy and her whole crowd, too," I explained. I said the part about Stacy softly, so that Michel wouldn't hear. "Then I had that fight with Mom and Jean-Paul, and I didn't think *I* was even going. And now it's kind of late."

Actually, Laurel had been really nice to me even before finding out about the playoff party. I kind of felt badly that I didn't invite her, but I really wanted just my best friends to be there.

Emily pulled into her space in our five-car garage. I noticed that Jean-Paul's black Mercedes was already parked there.

"Jean-Paul is home early," I said, glancing at my watch. "It's only three-thirty."

Michel nodded. "*Oui.* Mom told me this morning that my father is working only half a day. He wants to check out the viewing box for the party at the arena. Then we have to buy balloons and streamers. He's getting Cook to make a few salads and cookies and brownies to bring along. He's also ordered two of those yard-long hero sandwiches to be delivered to our viewing box from a deli near the arena. This is very cool, no?"

I spun around to look at Michel in the backseat. Since when had he started calling my mother "Mom"? He had always called her "Eileen" before. I looked to see if Emily had noticed, but she was already halfway out the car door.

"K.C., are you coming?" Michel asked, waiting outside the car.

I just nodded and followed him to the front door. Mrs. Smith, dressed in her usual black skirt and crisp white blouse, opened the door for the three of us.

"Good afternoon," she greeted us pleasantly. "Mr. Beauvais would like to see you in his study."

Jean-Paul has his own office off the library. It has a private phone line, a computer, and even a fax machine so he can do work at home and not have to stay at his office in Minneapolis so late.

"I'll be there in a sec!" Emily called as she hurried up the stairs. I knew she was going to her room to call Reed. She was *always* calling Reed.

"*Très bien. Merci,* Mrs. Smith," Michel said. He dropped his book bag on the floor of the foyer and made a beeline for his dad's office.

Mrs. Smith stooped and picked up his bag. "May I take your books up to your room, Miss Katie? Mr. Beauvais wants to see you, too."

I was about to say that I would take the books myself later, but she had already taken my knapsack out of my hand. I guess she had to go upstairs to Michel's room anyway. "Thank you," I told her.

I took my time going to Jean-Paul's office. I had a bad feeling about this. Why did Jean-Paul want to see me, Michel, and Emily? Well, at least Mom's car wasn't in the garage. If she wasn't home yet, then maybe I wasn't going to get in trouble now.

I walked through the library and into Jean-Paul's wood-paneled office. Jean-Paul sat in a burgundy leather chair behind his oak desk, and Michel was just going over to give him a big hug.

"*Papa! Merci beaucoup!*" Michel said. When he saw me, he said, "K.C., look! Isn't it *incroyable?*" He held up what looked like a Minnesota Wingers jersey.

"Wow!" I said, looking at the blue-and-yellow jersey. "Is that an official one?"

Jean-Paul nodded. "I have ones for you and Emily, too," he told me, taking two more jerseys out of his desk drawer. "I didn't have anything put on the back of yours because I didn't know what name you wanted on it," he added.

Looking at Michel's jersey, I noticed that it had "BEAUVAIS" written across the back where the player's name usually is.

All of a sudden it hit me. Jean-Paul wanted Emily and me to take his name!

I had never even thought about what it would be like to be Katie Beauvais. I had always been Katie Campbell. I would definitely have to talk to Emily about this.

I leaned across the desk and took the shirt from him. "Thank you very much, Jean-Paul. It's fine the way it is," I said, glancing at the empty space on the back of the shirt.

"All right. But if you decide to put something on the back, just tell me," Jean-Paul said, smiling at me. Then he dropped the subject.

"Okay. Thanks again," I said. I didn't know what else to say, so I just stood there holding the jersey in one hand.

"Papa, did you get the decorations for the party?" Michel asked. I was really relieved that he had broken the uncomfortable silence between Jean-Paul and me.

"*Oui*. Blue and yellow balloons and streamers, just like you asked," Jean-Paul told him. "Are you all set to help Eileen and me decorate tomorrow?"

"Of course!" Michel replied. "Maybe I'll invite a few of the guys to help, too."

Looking from Michel to me, Jean-Paul said, "Katie, will you be at the party?" I realized that it was only yesterday that I had run out of the room crying that I wasn't going to the party at all.

"Yes," I said quietly, letting my eyes drop.

"*Très bien*. You and your friends are welcome to come early and help us decorate, if you like," Jean-Paul added.

"Okay, thanks," I told him. "I'm going to call Sabrina and tell her about my jersey," I said, turning to leave.

"Oh, Katie — wait!" said Jean-Paul. When I turned back to him, he told me, "Your mother called. She won't be home for dinner tonight. She has a late meeting, so it will be just us."

"Oh, okay," I said. Then I left the room. I was on my way up the main stairs when Emily passed me on her way down.

"So, what does Jean-Paul want?" she asked me, stopping on the stairs.

"He got us a present," I said, holding up the jersey.

"Oh, great! Maybe I'll give mine to Reed. He'll freak over it," Emily said. Then she continued down the stairs.

I figured Emily didn't have to decide which name to put on her jersey if she was giving it to Reed. I decided not to worry about that right now, though.

Running the rest of the way up to my room, I sat on my bed and dialed the princess phone on my night table. I had to admit it was pretty neat having a phone in my room. I didn't have a private line like Emily, but it was cool having a phone just the same.

"Hello?" Sabs answered the phone on the

fourth ring, out of breath. Her bedroom is in the attic and the phone is on the first floor, so she has to run down the two flights of stairs to answer it.

"Hi, Sabs. Let me guess, you were up in your room," I said into the receiver.

"Hi, Katie! How'd you know?" Sabs asked. "Oh, never mind. Did you decide what to wear to the party yet?"

I took a deep breath. Sabs was going to die when she heard this! "I'm going to wear my very own official Wingers uniform jersey!" I shouted over the line.

"Awesome! Where did you get that?"

"Jean-Paul brought it home for me," I answered. "Michel and Emily each have one, too."

"You must be totally excited," Sabs told me. "Wait — I know, you can wear it with blue jeans, yellow socks, and your blue Keds!"

"Good idea, Sabs," I said. "Maybe you guys can wear blue and yellow, too."

"Right! We'll be like team mascots," Sabs said excitedly. "I'm going to get off right now and see if I can find something that's blue and yellow to wear. Then I have to call Randy and Al and tell them."

"Okay, Sabs. Oh, and if you guys want to come early tomorrow, we're going to start decorating the box at the arena around five-thirty," I told her.

We said good-bye, and then I put the receiver back in its cradle. Since it was Friday, I didn't have too much homework — just some math problems and a social studies chapter to read. An hour and a half later, I was done.

The night went pretty fast. Michel and I played a game of pool and then it was time to eat. Dinner was kind of uncomfortable. Emily had gone out to eat with Reed, so it was only Michel, Jean-Paul, and me. I was still feeling kind of weird about Jean-Paul. I mean, I had been really mean to him yesterday, but he was being nicer than ever to me. I also had to think about the name thing.

Mom got home after nine o'clock and was really tired, so she just went up to her bedroom. I was starting to think maybe she wasn't ever going to talk to me about how I'd behaved to Jean-Paul.

I went to bed before ten so I could get up early in the morning and get ready for the party.

I fell asleep right away, but then I had a nightmare about the hockey party. There were hundreds of kids there, crammed into one little viewing booth. I couldn't even see out the window to watch the game!

Then everyone there began to call my name. Even the strangers in the stands were calling, "Katie! Katie!" Then I was on the ice, wearing my jersey and playing left wing for the Wingers, and Scottie and Michel were on the ice with me.

I was about to pass the puck to Michel, but he was too busy talking to Stacy and didn't see me. I went to pass to Scottie, but he was rolling on the ice, laughing. Then I realized I had that mud mask on again and everyone was laughing at me!

Then suddenly I woke up. My heart was pounding really fast. Staring through the darkness at the outline of the white lace canopy above my head, I tried to calm down. Sometimes even the weirdest dreams can seem real in the middle of the night. Seeing Pepper curled up in a tiny ball of fur at the end of my bed made me feel a little better, though.

I glanced at the red digital numbers on the

clock next to my bed. It was 3:30 A.M. Somehow
I knew I wouldn't be able to fall back to sleep
right away. Maybe a glass of milk and one of
Cook's oatmeal cookies would help.

I swung my legs over the edge of the bed
and lowered my feet onto the soft carpet. By
the light of my nightlight, I found my robe and
slippers and went out to the hall. Ever since I
was little, Mom has always left a small light on
in the hall. That was one thing that *hadn't*
changed in the new house, so I had no problem
finding the back stairs.

When I got to the bottom of the stairs, I
noticed a light on in the kitchen. Cook must
have forgotten to shut it off after she'd cleaned
up the kitchen. I walked into the room and then
stopped short with a gasp.

"Katie! I'm sorry if I scared you," Jean-Paul
said softly.

For the second time tonight my heart was
pounding. I definitely had not been expecting to
see Jean-Paul sitting at the kitchen table in the
middle of the night.

"I couldn't sleep," I finally managed to say. I
guess he couldn't sleep, either. He was sitting
there in his red silk robe with a plate of cookies

and a glass of milk in front of him.

"Please, help yourself," he said, gesturing to the pitcher of milk on the table.

I was torn between wanting to run upstairs and wanting to tell him I was sorry and talk about everything that had been going on lately.

I decided I had to at least apologize to him. "Thanks," I said. I opened the cabinet door and took out a glass. Jean-Paul poured me a glass of milk as I took a cookie. I noticed that he had dark circles under his eyes and looked really tired.

I was trying to think of what to say to Jean-Paul when he looked at me and asked softly, "Katie, can we talk?"

I looked up at him and nodded, but then avoided his eyes.

"I know you haven't been very happy lately and I can only guess it's because of me," Jean-Paul began.

I kept my eyes down and listened.

"Everything has happened very quickly. I knew it would be hard for you to get used a new father and brother, so I've done everything I can to make you happy. But still, I feel . . ."

Jean-Paul didn't finish his sentence, but I

knew exactly what he meant. I hadn't been very nice to him lately.

"What can I do?" Jean-Paul said after a pause. "What can I do to make you like me, Katie?"

Looking up at him, I said, "I do like you, Jean-Paul. The problem is, I mean you've done too much!" I tried to explain.

He shook his head, looking really confused. "Too much?"

"Like buying this house," I began.

"But your old house was so small, and my condo was even smaller," Jean-Paul said.

"I know, but did you have to buy the biggest house in Acorn Falls?" I blurted out.

Somehow this wasn't going as I had planned. All I had wanted to do was apologize and leave. But here I was telling Jean-Paul all the things he had done wrong! I remembered what Emily had said about telling people when things bother me and not just holding them in. But I didn't know if that was the right thing to be doing *now*.

Jean-Paul sat there looking at me. Then he took a deep breath and said, "Katie, when I was very young, younger than you and Michel, my family was very poor. My father had struggled to pay for college, hoping it would help him to get a better job than his father, who was a poor fisherman."

My mouth fell open. It was hard to imagine that Jean-Paul had ever been poor.

"He began a company and for the first five years, never took a penny for himself," Jean-Paul went on. "My mother had to baby-sit and do other people's housework so we could buy clothes to wear. Finally the company grew and my father started to make some money.

"Now that company, my company, is the biggest advertising company in Canada and the third biggest in Minneapolis. That is why I bought the biggest house in Acorn Falls. I never want my children to ever have to want for anything. I want the best for you and your mother. I'm sorry we didn't consult you first, but we were so sure you would be pleased," Jean-Paul explained. "Don't you like the house?"

I tried to find the right words to explain how I felt.

"Yes, but . . . it's so far from school. It's a pain to have Emily pick me up all the time, and

I can't walk to my friends' houses anymore," I told him. Suddenly, after the story Jean-Paul had told me about his childhood, all my excuses for not liking the house seemed really silly and selfish.

Jean-Paul nodded. "I understand. Tomorrow, I'll hire a chauffeur to drive you and Michel to school and to your friends' houses whenever you want. Then Emily won't have to bother. I should have thought of it before."

At first I thought he was kidding, but then I looked at his face and realized he was perfectly serious. "No! I mean, that's another thing. I don't want everyone at school to think that we're rich!" I cried.

Jean-Paul chuckled softly. "But, Katie, we *are* rich."

"I don't want everyone at school to think I'm a snob! I mean, we already have servants." I realized I had whispered the words like it was an embarrassing secret.

"Katie, when you learn more about people, you'll realize something," Jean-Paul told me. "Just because someone has money doesn't mean they think they are better than everyone else."

I thought about that for a minute and realized he was right. After all, Jean-Paul and Michel never acted snobby, and they were very rich.

"So, now tell me why you didn't want to come to the playoff party tomorrow afternoon, and why you were so upset yesterday when that girl Stacy Hansen was here," Jean-Paul asked.

"Everybody at school wants tickets —" I began.

"I can get you as many tickets as you want, Katie," Jean-Paul interrupted me. "Don't be afraid to ask me."

"That's not the problem," I said quickly. He really didn't understand what was going on at school at all. I remembered what Emily had said about him and Michel not being mind readers. I should have told him from the beginning what I felt.

"There are people at school that I don't even know who bother me for tickets," I started over. "Then there are people who never wanted to be my friends until you bought the Wingers, and now they act like we're best buddies!"

"Like Stacy?" Jean-Paul guessed.

I looked up at him in surprise. "Yes."

"I'm sorry, Katie," he said. "I should have realized what was going on. But Stacy did come over with those flowers as a housewarming present for your mother, and she seemed to be very friendly with Michel."

I frowned. "That's what I'm afraid of. Stacy tried to be nice to me the day after the Wingers got into the playoffs. I know her too well to fall for it, but Michel doesn't know what a rotten person she is!"

Jean-Paul took a sip of his milk. "Did you talk to Michel about how you feel about Stacy?" he asked.

I looked down at my hands again. "No."

"Maybe you should," Jean-Paul suggested.

I nodded.

"And maybe you should talk to him about bringing the hockey team into the house, or the bathroom, without telling you first," Jean-Paul continued. "He's not used to having girls in the house. It's only been the two of us for a long time now."

I nodded again.

"Is there anything else bothering you?" Jean-Paul asked.

"Yes," I began. Tears sprang to my eyes, and

Jean-Paul waited patiently while I blinked a few times and swallowed. "I want to apologize for being so horrible lately. I'm sorry."

Jean-Paul smiled. "You're forgiven."

"Now all I have to do is get Mom to forgive me," I said, grabbing another cookie. Suddenly I realized how hungry I was.

"Don't worry about your mother. I think she understands how hard all these changes have been for you. She loves you very much and just wants you to be happy," Jean-Paul offered.

I smiled at him. "I know," I said, feeling a little sheepish. "But Jean-Paul, thanks for the party and the jersey and . . . for everything."

Suddenly Jean-Paul didn't look tired at all. He just squeezed my hand and said good night.

Chapter Eleven

I woke up pretty late on Saturday morning, probably because I had been up for a while the night before, talking to Jean-Paul. I have to say, it felt really good to get things straightened out with him.

I got out of bed and stretched. Then I slowly made my way into the bathroom. It felt wonderful to take a nice long shower. When I was done, I dried my hair with the blow dryer that was attached to the wall in the bathroom.

I went back in my room to get dressed. I had just finished pulling on my jeans when Jean-Paul came over the intercom and said brunch was ready. Jean-Paul makes breakfast for us now only on the weekends, because the cook has Saturday and Sunday off.

When I entered the dining room, Jean-Paul smiled at me, and I smiled back. Things definitely felt better. I heard Mom talking on the phone in the foyer and she sounded like she was in a great mood, too. I guess Jean-Paul had told her about our talk earlier this morning.

Brunch tasted especially good. I wondered if it was because I was starving or because I felt better about Jean-Paul. Anyway, he had made Belgian waffles and apple puff pancakes, along with plenty of bacon and sausage and fresh-squeezed orange juice.

We were almost finished eating when the phone rang. Mom answered and told Michel he had a call. Michel talked for a few minutes and then came back shaking his head.

"*Mon Dieu!* That Stacy is so strange. She wanted to know what I was wearing to the playoff party," Michel said, then looked embarrassed. "I'm sorry, I know she is your friend, Katie."

I stared at Michel. "*My* friend? I thought *you* liked her!" I cried.

Michel shook his head. "I was only nice to her because I thought she was *your* friend! I did wonder why she was so mean sometimes to you and your friends." He started to crack up, and before I knew it, we were both laughing. Thinking about all the things Stacy had said and done *was* kind of funny.

Jean-Paul raised his eyebrows and looked at Mom. She just smiled back at Jean-Paul, and soon they started to laugh. Things were definitely starting to work out!

After brunch I ran upstairs to my room to get ready for the party and game. The sun was shining through my bedroom windows, and my room really did look pretty. Opening the door to my walk-in closet, I stared at the mostly empty racks. I didn't think I would ever have enough clothes to fill them up. No one would ever need that many clothes.

I put on my Wingers jersey over a yellow turtleneck that matched the color of the writing on the blue jersey. Then I pulled on my blue jeans, a pair of yellow socks, and my dark blue sneakers.

I went over to the full-length oak swivel mirror and looked at my reflection. Sabs was right. This outfit matched perfectly.

A moment later, there was a knock on the door between the bathroom and my room.

"Come in," I called. It could only be Michel unless there was a stranger in our bathroom.

Michel opened the door and stood in the

doorway modeling his Wingers jersey. He had tucked the jersey into a faded pair of jeans. The yellow stripe on his white Nike hightops matched the Wingers letters. He looked really cool.

"*Magnifique!* You look great, K.C. Are you ready to go?" Michel asked.

"Yup," I replied. I had just pulled my hair back into a dark blue ponytail holder. "Let's go!"

The drive to Minneapolis seemed to take forever, but it was only about an hour. Finally, we pulled up to the back of the arena in Jean-Paul's Mercedes. Emily followed in her car with Reed and Ron.

Jean-Paul parked the car in a space marked "Reserved for J. P. Beauvais." For the first time I began to realize just how influential he was and what it meant to own one of the best hockey teams in the world!

We had just finished unloading all of the salads and cookies that Cook had made, and had started setting them out on tables in the room, when Sabs, Randy, and Al walked in. All three of them were wearing blue and yellow, too, and they looked really great.

"Wow! Look at this!" Sabs cried. She ran to the huge glass windows of the owner's box, which looked right out over the rink.

"Best seats in the house!" said Randy, going to stand next to Sabs.

Allison turned to me and asked, "So what can we do to help?"

I handed her a roll of yellow streamers. "Lots. We only have an hour before everyone gets here."

Scottie and Brian showed up soon, and with everyone's help, we got the box decorated and looking great in less than an hour. Mom and Emily set out the buffet of food that had been delivered from the deli in Minneapolis. And Jean-Paul, Reed, and Ron carried in pails of ice and soda from the arena's concession stands.

Before we knew it, kids from school started to arrive. Billy Dixon, Sam, Jason, Arizonna, and Nick came in a big group. Then some more of the guys on the Bradley hockey team came in.

"I wonder when Stacy and Eva are going to show up?" Sabs asked, raising an eyebrow at Al and Randy.

"Eva's coming, too?" I asked.

Randy nodded. "Yeah, I heard Stacy talking. She claims she asked Michel and Jean-Paul if she could invite a friend, and they said yes."

I decided not to worry about it. "I guess it doesn't matter," I told my friends. "Maybe she'll talk to Eva all night and leave us alone."

"Oh, I don't think we have to worry about her staying all night!" Sabs said, smiling.

"Are you guys *ever* going to tell me what you're up to?" I asked.

Just then Al pointed to the door. "You're about to find out," she told me.

I spun around. There in the doorway stood Stacy and Eva. Stacy was dressed in a tight green mermaid outfit that she could barely walk in. Eva stood next to her in a lobster outfit, claws and all!

"Ohmygosh!" I cried. "What did you guys do?"

"We told her it was a costume party!" Sabs told me. She was holding her hand over her mouth to keep from laughing.

"So *that's* why she called Michel this morning to ask what he was wearing," I exclaimed. I couldn't help it. I started to laugh, too.

Just then Ben Mulberry, the star forward for

the Wingers, walked in behind Stacy. He also happens to be one of the cutest hockey players alive. "Great! Entertainment!" he said when he saw Stacy and Eva.

Stacy's face turned even redder than the color of Eva's lobster costume. She spun around and nearly fell over trying to get out of the room in her mermaid outfit. Eva grabbed Stacy's arm, and they hobbled out of the room and down the hall.

Everyone in the room started laughing really hard.

"That was hysterical!" Randy said. She was laughing so hard that she was crying.

"Katherine Campbell! Did you have anything to do with this?" Mom's stern voice said right behind me.

I turned around slowly. Seeing Mom's angry face kind of took the fun out of the joke that my friends had played on Stacy and Eva.

"No, Mom, I swear! I had no idea!" I told her.

"It was our fault, Mrs. Beauvais," Randy said, going over to my mom. Al and Sabs were right with her.

"The whole thing was my idea," Sabs added.

"I'm sorry, Mrs. Beauvais."

"My friends and I helped, too," Sam put in. His freckled face turned bright red as he stepped up next to his sister.

Just then Jean-Paul came over and took my mother's hand, pulling her close to him. "Come on, *ma chérie*. Give the kids a break. It *was* a little mean, but from what I've heard about Stacy, she deserved it. Maybe this will teach her to be nicer."

Mom's face softened a little. "Well, okay. But you girls must never play a trick like that on anyone again," she warned us. "And I don't want this to be the big joke at school next week."

. "Don't worry, Mom," I said quickly."

"Jean-Paul is so cool!" Sabs said after my mother walked away.

"He gives a great party, too!" said Randy.

"It's not just the party," Allison added. "Jean-Paul saved us all from getting in real trouble with Katie's mom."

My friends were right. Jean-Paul was totally cool. Suddenly I was really proud to have him as my new father. "I'll be right back," I said.

A lot of the Wingers had arrived, so it took

me a few minutes to get across the crowded room to Jean-Paul.

"Hello, Katie. Are you and your friends having a good time?" Jean-Paul asked.

I grinned at him. "We're having a great time! Thank you so much for the party. And for not getting mad about what my friends did to Stacy."

"*De rien,*" he said with a smile. "It's nothing. But your mother is right. This is the type of thing you must never do again."

I nodded my head in agreement. "Jean-Paul, there's something else I want to thank you for," I went on.

"*Oui?*" Jean-Paul asked, looking at me expectantly.

I leaned over to hug him and said, "Thanks for my new family."

Jean-Paul didn't say anything — he just beamed.

Don't miss
GIRL TALK #20:
ROCKIN' CLASS TRIP

"This is a private conversation," I said loudly without even turning around. I just knew it was that stuck-up Stacy Hansen who had sneaked up behind me. She's the principal's phony-baloney daughter.

"Well, don't flatter yourselves into thinking we came here to talk to you drones," Stacy haughtily informed us.

"Actually, my concert tickets just flew off my tray and landed right under Sabrina's seat here," she chatted matter-of-factly, as she bent down under my chair. "I just came here to get them." Stacy said, flipping her hair behind her.

"And we wouldn't want to lose *these babies*," Eva chimed in. "Because you know how impossible it is to get Dylan Palmer tickets."

"Dylan Palmer!" I excitedly yelped and bolted straight out of my chair, knocking it back onto Stacy's head. For a minute, it seemed like the whole cafeteria froze and turned to look in our direction.

"You've got tickets to the Dylan Palmer concert in Minneapolis! That's impossible!" I breathlessly exclaimed. And I was sorry as soon as I said the words. It was just the reaction Stacy was looking for.

But you have to understand, Dylan Palmer is my *absolute* favorite rock star of all time. I would give just about anything to see him in person. ANYTHING! The tickets were for next weekend, and as far as I knew, they had been sold out for weeks. I just couldn't believe she got them.

"Are you sure you've got all five?" B.Z. sarcastically asked, peering over Stacy's shoulder.

Stacy innocently widened her eyes and deliberately fanned the tickets out in front of her face.

"One . . . two . . . three . . . four . . . five," she slowly counted out loud. "That's five Dylan Palmer tickets, front row and center, all accounted for," she drooled in a sugary sweet tone.

"Front row and center," I involuntarily mumbled under my breath, along with about twenty other kids. I thought I was going to die right there on the spot.

"But you know Eva," Stacy continued as if there were no one else around, "I've got five tickets here . . . and there's only four of us."

Suddenly the whole crowd seemed to lurch forward at the same time. Everyone seemed to be holding their breath, hanging on for Stacy's next word.

"Tell me, Stacy," Randy cut in. "Did you guys rehearse this, or do you just improvise as you go along? Don't you think they deserve a hand for a great performance?" Randy announced, turning to the crowd and clapping her hands.

"You're going to wish you never said that, Randy Zak!" Stacy fumed, trying to compose herself.

"YOU WISH!" Randy retorted. "You think you're such a big shot with your front row tickets. Well, let me tell you, Stacy Hansen . . . nobody cares."

As soon as Randy said, "nobody cares," I tried to focus my eyes on the floor.

"I know one person who cares," Stacy slowly said. And when she said it, I knew she was staring right at me.

LOOK FOR THE AWESOME GIRL TALK BOOKS IN A STORE NEAR YOU!

Fiction

Nonfiction

ASK ALLIE: 101 answers to your questions about boys, friends, family, and school!

YOUR PERSONALITY QUIZ: Fun, easy quizzes to help you discover the real you!

TALK BACK!

TELL US WHAT YOU THINK ABOUT GIRL TALK

Name _____

Address _____

City _____ State _____ Zip _____

Birthday Day _____ Mo. _____ Year _____

Telephone Number (____) _____

1) On a scale of 1 (The Pits) to 5 (The Max), how would you rate Girl Talk?   Circle One:

1   2   3   4   5

2) What do you like most about Girl Talk?

___Characters___Situations___Telephone Talk

Other _____

3) Who is your favorite character? Circle One:

Sabrina   Katie   Randy

Allison   Stacy   Other

4) Who is your least favorite character?

_____

5) What do you want to read about in Girl Talk?

_____

_____

Send completed form to :
Western Publishing Company, Inc.
1220 Mound Avenue Mail Station #85
Racine, Wisconsin 53404